She needed to tell him—needed to be honest with him about the little she did remember. But before she could open her mouth, his lips pressed against hers.

And whatever thoughts she'd had fled her mind. She couldn't think at all. She could only feel. Desire overwhelmed her. Her skin tingled and her pulse raced.

He kissed her with all the passion she felt for him.

Then his palms cupped her face, cradling the cheek she'd touched looking for a scar. And he pulled back.

"I'm sorry," he apologized, and his broad shoulders slumped as if he'd added to that load of guilt and regret he already carried. "I shouldn't have done that...."

"Why did you?" she wondered aloud. With a bruised face and ugly scrubs stretched taut over her big belly, she was hardly desirable.

Those broad shoulders lifted but then dropped again in a slight shrug. "I wanted you to remember me—to remember what we once were to each other."

LISA CHILDS

PROTECTING THE PREGNANT PRINCESS

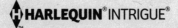

HARLEQUIN® INTRIGUE®

For my parents, Jack and Mary Lou Childs. Alzheimer's disease has
stolen her memories of their long life together, but he is still her hero—
loving and protecting her. While her mind doesn't always remember
him, her heart will never forget that he is the love of her life.

ISBN-13: 978-0-373-69670-3

Recycling programs
for this product may
not exist in your area.

PROTECTING THE PREGNANT PRINCESS

Copyright © 2013 by Lisa Childs

HARLEQUIN®

Printed in U.S.A.

™ www.Harlequin.com

ABOUT THE AUTHOR

Bestselling, award-winning author Lisa Childs writes paranormal and contemporary romance for Harlequin Books. She lives on thirty acres in west Michigan with her two daughters, a talkative Siamese and a long-haired Chihuahua who thinks she's a rottweiler. Lisa loves hearing from readers, who can contact her through her website, www.lisachilds.com, or snail-mail address, P.O. Box 139, Marne, MI 49435.

Books by Lisa Childs

CAST OF CHARACTERS

Aaron Timmer—The royal bodyguard has to protect the princess, her memory and his heart from falling for another woman he might lose.

Charlotte Green—She's the doppelganger bodyguard of Princess St. Pierre who will do anything to protect the woman—even take her place in danger.

Princess Gabriella St. Pierre—The royal heiress has been in danger since the day she was born and the threats to her life put everyone around her in danger—no one more than Charlotte.

Whitaker Howell—Aaron's fellow royal bodyguard who has betrayed him before.

King St. Pierre—The royal monarch will not tolerate betrayal or disobedience from anyone—even his family.

Centerenian—Under another's orders, he kidnapped the princess. Or so he thinks...

Jason "Trigger" Herrema—The U.S. Marshal is Charlotte Green's former partner who has his own agenda for helping Aaron find her.

Prince Linus Demetrius—The former fiancé of Princess Gabriella doesn't accept their broken engagement with grace.

Stanley Jessup—The media mogul offers Aaron a lead but he has more reasons to hurt Aaron than to help him.

Prologue

Heat scorched his face and hands, but Aaron Timmer ignored the pain and ran headlong toward the fire. His breath whooshed out of his burning lungs as his body dropped, tackled to the ground.

"You damn fool, what the hell are you thinking?" asked the man who'd knocked him down.

"We have to save her!" As her bodyguards, saving her was their responsibility. But she had become more than just a job to Aaron.

"It's too late." The house—the *safe* house—they had stashed her in was fully engulfed. The roof was gone, and flames were rising up toward the trees overhead. Leaves caught fire, dissolving into sparks that rained down onto the blackened lawn surrounding the house.

"We shouldn't have left her." But Aaron's partner, Whitaker Howell, had insisted that she would be fine— that no one could have possibly figured out where she was.

Obviously someone had.

He rolled over and swung his fist right into Whit's hard jaw. His knuckles cracked and stung as blood oozed from them. He shook off the pain and pushed away Whit's limp body. Then he turned back to the burning frame of the house, debris strewn wide around the yard from the explosion.

It was too late. She was gone.

Three years later...

BLOOD SPATTERED THE ivory brocade walls of the Parisian hotel suite. Holes were torn through the paper, causing plaster and insulation to spill onto the hardwood floor. Some of the holes were big, probably from a fist or a foot; others smaller and blackened with gunpowder. The glass in the windows was broken, the frames splintered. Shots had been fired. And there had been one hell of a struggle.

Aaron's heart hammered against his ribs, panic and fear overwhelming him as he surveyed the gruesome crime scene.

A whistle hissed through clenched teeth—not his but Whit's, the man with whom he'd vowed to never work again after that tragedy three years ago. But a couple of months ago he'd been offered an opportunity too good to pass up. Only after he'd accepted the position as a royal bodyguard had he learned that he was actually going to share that assignment with his former business partner and friend.

That safe house explosion had destroyed whatever bond they'd formed in war, fighting together in Afghanistan. After the fire, they had only fought each other. So Aaron should have walked away from this job. He should have known how it would end.

"She put up one hell of a fight," Whit said, his deep voice almost reverent with respect. "But there's no way they survived..."

Aaron shook his head, refusing to accept that they

were gone. *She* couldn't be gone. Charlotte Green was too strong and too smart to not have survived whatever had happened to her.

What the hell had happened to her?

To them? Charlotte Green was also a royal body-guard for the princess of St. Pierre Island, an affluent nation near Greece.

Aaron and Whit had retraced their steps from their missed flight home, back to the hotel they'd been booked into in Paris. The suite had been destroyed. But despite the amount of blood pooled on the hardwood floor, the Parisian authorities had found no bodies. No witnesses. No leads at all. And no hope for survivors.

King Rafael St. Pierre nodded in agreement with Whit Howell's statement of resignation. Aaron clenched his fists, wanting to punch both men in the face. He couldn't strike the king though, and not just because he was paid generously to protect the ruler of St. Pierre. He couldn't hurt the man because Rafael was already hurting so much that he probably wouldn't even feel the blow.

Whit, on the other hand…

For the past three years Aaron had wanted to do much more than just strike the man. He had damn sure never intended to work with him again. But when they'd both been hired, separately, to protect the king, neither had been willing to give up the job—a security job they'd been lucky to get after what had happened to the last person they'd protected together.

The king was fine, though. Physically. Emotionally, he was a wreck. The man, once fit and vital, was show-ing every year and then some of his age in the slump of his back and shoulders and in the gray that now liberally streaked his dark hair. Clearly Rafael St. Pierre was beside himself with grief.

Despite how far he and Whit went back, to a friendship forged under fire in Afghanistan, Aaron never knew exactly what his ex-business partner was thinking. Or feeling, or if Whit was even capable of feeling anything at all.

As dissimilar as they were physically, Whit being blond and dark-eyed and Aaron dark-haired with light blue eyes, they were even more unlike emotionally. Aaron was feeling too much; frustration, fear and grief battled for dominance inside him. But then anger swept aside those emotions, snapping his control. He shouted a question at both men, "How can you just give up?"

Whit's head snapped back, as if Aaron had slugged him. And the king flinched, his naturally tan complexion fading to a pasty white that made him look as dead as he believed his daughter and her female bodyguard to be.

Whit glanced at the king, as if worried that the once so powerful man might keel over and die. They could protect the ruler from a bullet but not a heart attack. Or a broken heart. Whit turned back to Aaron, his intense stare a silent warning for him to control his temper.

He had to speak his mind. "Charlotte Green is the best damn bodyguard I've ever worked with." Before she'd gone into private duty protection, she had been a U.S. Marshal. "She could have fought them off. She could have protected them both. She devoted herself to protecting the princess. She went above and beyond the responsibilities of her job."

And to extremes that no other guard could have or would have gone.

"It isn't just a job to her," Aaron continued, his throat

thick with emotion as thoughts of Charlotte pummeled him. Her beauty. Her brains. Her loyal heart. "She considers Princess Gabriella a friend."

"That's why she would have died *for* her," Whit pointed out, "and why she must have died *with* her."

Aaron's heart lurched in his chest. "No..."

"If they were alive, we would have heard from them by now," Whit insisted. "They would have reached out to us or the palace."

Unless they didn't think they could trust them, unless they felt betrayed. Maybe that was why it was easier for Whit and the king to accept their deaths; it was easier than accepting their own responsibility for the young women's disappearances.

"No matter how fierce a fighter she was," Whit said, "Charlotte Green is gone. She's dead. And if the princess was alive, we would have had a ransom demand by now."

The king gasped but then nodded in agreement.

Aaron shook his head. "No. We need to keep looking. They have to be out there—somewhere." He couldn't have been too late again. Charlotte Green couldn't be gone.

Chapter One

Six months later...

Like a sledgehammer shattering her skull, pain throbbed inside her head—clouding her mind. She couldn't think. She could barely feel...anything but that incessant pain. Even her hair hurt, and her skin felt stretched, as if pulled taut over a bump. She moved her fingers to touch her head, but she couldn't lift her hand.

Something bound her wrist—not so tightly that it hurt like her skull hurt, but she couldn't budge her hand. Either hand. She tugged at both and found that her wrists were held down to something hard and cold.

She forced open her eyes and then squinted against the glare of the fluorescent lights burning brightly overhead. Dark spots blurred her vision. She blinked over and over in an attempt to clear her vision. But images remained distorted. To her it looked like she had six arms—all of them bound to railings of a bed like an octopus strapped down to a boat deck. A giggle bubbled up with a surge of hysteria, but the slight sound nearly shattered her skull.

The questions nagging at her threatened to finish the job. *What the hell happened to me? Where am I?* Because she had no answers...

She also had no idea why she was being held down—restrained like a criminal. Or a captive…

She fought against the overwhelming fear. She needed to focus, but her head wouldn't stop pounding and the pain almost blinded her, like the fluorescent light glaring down from the ceiling. It was unrelenting, and reminded her of the light in an interrogation room or torture chamber.

That light was all she could discern of her surroundings. Flinching against its glare, she looked down, but she couldn't see more than a couple of feet in front of her—not because of the pain but because she couldn't see beyond the mound of her belly.

Shock turned her giggle into a sharp gasp. *I'm pregnant?*

No…

Her swollen belly must have been like her seeing six hands, just distorted and out of focus. She wasn't pregnant…

In denial of the possibility, she shook her head, but the motion magnified her pain. She closed her eyes against the wave of agony and confusion that rushed over her, making her nauseous. Or was that sick feeling because of the pregnancy?

How far along was she? When had it happened? And with whom?

She gasped again, her breath leaving her lungs completely. Not only couldn't she remember who the father of her unborn child might be but she couldn't even remember who *she* was.

AARON HELD OUT his phone to check his caller ID, surprised at where the call was coming from. Sure, as desperate as he'd been he'd reached out to everyone he thought might be able to help. He had called Charlotte's ex-partner with the U.S. Marshals. He'd tried calling her aunt, but there must not have been any cell reception in whatever jungle she was building schools or orphanages. And he'd called this man...

"Hello, Mr. Jessup." This man was America's version of royalty—the ruler of an empire of news networks and magazines and newspapers. Nothing happened anywhere without his knowing about it—unless a more powerful man, like King St. Pierre, had covered it up. "Thank you for calling me back."

Aaron was surprised that the man would speak to him at all. He was the last client of the security firm in which Aaron and Whit had been partners. He had hired them to protect the most important thing to him. And they had failed...

"Don't thank me yet," the older man warned him. "Not until you see if the lead pans out."

"You have a lead?"

"Someone called in a tip from a private sanatorium in northern Michigan, wanting to sell a story about Princess Gabriella St. Pierre being committed to the psychiatric facility."

From that destroyed hotel room to a private sanatorium? Given what she'd seen, what she must have gone through, it almost made sense. A tip like this was why Aaron had refused to give up. That and a feeling deep in his gut—maybe his heart—that told him Charlotte Green wasn't dead. She couldn't be dead—somehow he'd know if she was.

"Is she alone?" he asked.

"She's got a royal entourage," Jessup said, "including a private doctor and nurse."

Royal? But the king swore he knew nothing of their

disappearance. And a man couldn't feign the kind of grief he was obviously experiencing.

"And a security detail?" Aaron asked. Or at least one very strong woman.

Stanley Jessup grunted. "Yeah, too much of it according to the source."

Hope fluttered in Aaron's chest. Was it possible? Had he found them both? "Is one of the guards a woman?"

"I don't know." The man sighed. "I'm getting this third hand—from the editor of a magazine who got it from an ambitious young reporter. I don't have details yet, but I'm going to check it out."

"Why?" The question slipped out.

Stanley Jessup grunted again, probably around the cigar he usually had clamped between his teeth. "It's a story—a damn good one since it involves royalty."

If only Stanley knew the real story…

But the women had been checked into that Parisian hotel under aliases. To prevent the paparazzi from hounding the princess, Charlotte had developed several alternative identities for them. She had been that thorough and that good.

Still was—she couldn't be dead. Aaron had already lost one woman he thought he might have been falling for—Stanley Jessup's daughter.

"Why call me?" Aaron asked the newsman. "Why talk to me at all?"

"I don't blame you or Whit for what happened three years ago," Jessup assured him. "Neither should you."

Stanley, despite grieving for his daughter, might have found a way to absolve them of any culpability. But Aaron hadn't.

"Do you want me to call you back after I get more details?" Stanley asked. "I'm going to talk to this young reporter to verify he really has a source inside the sanatorium. Then I'll see if he can get a picture to prove it's actually her."

"No," Aaron replied. He couldn't trust anyone else to do that. No one else would know for certain which woman she really was. "Just tell me the name of this psychiatric hospital."

"Serenity House," Stanley divulged freely. "I'm going to have that reporter follow up with his source, too, Aaron. Anything Princess Gabby does is newsworthy, and this story is a hell of a lot more exciting than her attending a fashion show or movie premiere. And she hasn't even hit one of those in a few months— maybe longer. In fact, she's kind of dropped off the face of the earth."

Or so everyone had believed. But if it really was her...

"I know I don't have any right to ask you for a favor..."

"You said that when you called the first time," Jessup reminded him, "when you asked me if I'd heard anything recently about the princess."

"So I definitely don't have any right to ask you for a second favor," Aaron amended himself.

"That's BS," Stanley replied with a snort of disgust. "You can ask me anything, but I have the right to refuse if you're going to ask what I think you are."

"I'm not asking you *not* to run with the story," Aaron assured the man. He knew Stanley Jessup too well to ask that. "I'm just asking you to run in place until I get there."

"So hold off on printing anything?"

"Just until I get there and personally confirm if it's really Princess Gabriella."

Stanley snorted again. "Since she was ten years old, Princess Gabriella St. Pierre's face has been everywhere—magazines, newspapers, entertainment magazines." Most of those he owned. "Everybody knows what her royal highness looks like."

Everyone did. But unfortunately she was no longer the only one who looked like her. The woman committed to the private sanatorium wasn't necessarily Princess Gabriella.

"Just hold off?" Aaron asked.

Stanley Jessup's sigh of resignation rattled the phone. "Sure."

"And one more favor—"

The older man chuckled. "So what's this? The third one now?"

"This is important," Aaron said. "I wouldn't have bothered you if it wasn't…" If Charlotte wasn't missing, he would have never been so insensitive as to contact Stanley Jessup again. He hated that probably just the sound of his voice reminded the man of all that he had lost: everything.

"I can tell that this is important to you," the older man replied. "So what's this third favor?"

Maybe the most important. "If Whit calls, don't tell him what you've told me."

"About the explosion not being his fault?"

Aaron snorted now. It had been Whit's fault; he'd convinced him that the safe house was really safe. That was why he couldn't trust another woman's safety to his former partner. "Don't tell him about Princess Gabriella."

"He'll read it for himself."

"Let him find out that way, and let *me* find out first if it's really the princess." Or Charlotte.

"You don't trust Whit?"

Not anymore. Whit had always cared more about the money than Aaron had. Maybe he cared too much. Maybe he'd been bought off—three years ago and now. Both times there must have been a man on the inside. Aaron hated to think that that man was one he'd once considered a friend—a man at whose side he'd fought. But war had changed so many veterans. Whit had changed. Maybe he'd gone from killing for his country to killing for the highest bidder.

"Promise me," Aaron beseeched his old client.

Jessup grunted. "You make it all sound so life and death. She's just a spoiled heiress who's probably been committed to this private hospital to get cleaned up or dried out."

Aaron had only interacted with the princess for a couple of months before her disappearance. Even at parties she'd never had more than a few sips of champagne and she had never appeared under the influence of drugs, either.

If this really was Princess Gabby at Serenity House, she wasn't there for rehab.

She stared at the stranger in the mirror above the bathroom sink. The woman had long—very long—caramel-brown hair hanging over her thin shoulders. And her face had delicate features and wide brown eyes. And a bruise on her temple that was fading from purple to yellow.

She lifted her hand and pressed her fingertips against the slightly swollen flesh. Pain throbbed yet inside her head, weakening her legs. She dropped both hands to the edge of the sink and held on until the dizziness passed. She needed to regain her strength, but even more she needed to regain her memory.

She didn't even recognize her own damn face in the mirror. "Who are you?" she asked that woman staring back at her through the glass. She needed a name—even if it wasn't her real one. She needed an identity. "Jane," she whispered. "Jane Doe."

Wasn't that what authorities called female amnesiacs…and unidentified *dead* female bodies?

Drawing in a shaky breath, *Jane* moved her hand from her head to her belly. Her flesh shifted beneath her palm, moving as something—*somebody*—moved inside her.

She didn't recognize her face or her body. What the hell was wrong with her? Maybe that was why she'd been locked up in this weird hospital/prison. Maybe it was for her own damn good. Her belly moved again as the baby kicked inside her, as if in protest of her thought.

"You want out of here, too," Jane murmured.

A fist hammered at the door, rattling the wood in the frame. The pounding rattled her brain inside her skull.

"Come out now, miss. You've been in there long enough."

The gruff command had her muscles tensing in protest and preparation for battle. But she was still too weak to fight.

The door had no lock, so it opened easily to the man who stood guard outside her room. Unlike the other hospital employees who wore scrubs, he wore a dark suit, and his black hair was oily and slicked back on his big, heavily featured head. His suit jacket shifted, revealing his holstered weapon. A Glock. As if familiar with the trigger, her fingers itched to grab for it.

But she would have to get close to the creep and if she got close, he could touch her, probably overpower her before she ever pulled the weapon from the holster. A cold chill chased down her spine, and she shivered in reaction.

A nurse moved around the guard. "You're cold," she said. "You need to get back into bed." The gray-haired woman wrapped an arm around Jane and helped her from the bathroom to the bed. The woman had a small, shiny metal nameplate pinned to her uniform shirt. *She* had a name: Sandy.

Jane found herself leaning heavily against the shorter woman. Her knees trembled, her legs turning into jelly in reaction to the short walk. With a tremulous sigh of relief she dropped onto the mattress.

"Put the restraints on her," the gruff-voiced guard ordered. He spoke with a heavy accent—some dialect she suspected she should have recognized if she could even recognize her own face right now.

"No, please," Jane implored the nurse, not the man. She doubted she could sway *him*. But the woman... "Sandy, please..."

The nurse turned toward the man, though. "Mr. Centerenian, do we have to? She's not strong enough to—"

"Put the restraints on her!" he snapped. "You remember what happened to her the last time you didn't..."

Deep red color flushed the woman's face and neck. But was her reaction in embarrassment or anger?

What had happened the last time Jane hadn't had on the restraints? She hadn't simply fallen out of bed...if that was what he was trying to imply.

Jane doubted the bruise on her head had come from a fall since she had no other corresponding bruises on her shoulder, arm or hip. At least not recent ones. But she had a plethora of fading bruises and even older scars.

More than likely the bruise on her face had come from a blow. She glanced again at the holster and the gun visible through Mr. Centerenian's open jacket. The handle of the Glock could have left such a bruise and bump on her temple. It also could have killed her.

From the loss of her memory and her strength, she suspected it nearly had. This man had attacked a pregnant woman? What kind of guard was he? He definitely wasn't there for her *protection*.

The nurse's hands trembled as she reached for the restraints that were attached to the bed railings.

"Sandy, please..." Jane implored her.

But the nurse wouldn't meet her gaze. She kept her head down, eyes averted, as she attached the strips of canvas and Velcro to Jane's wrists.

"Tight," the man ordered gruffly.

Sandy ripped loose the Velcro and readjusted the straps. But now the restraints felt even looser. The nurse snuck a quick, apologetic glance at Jane before turning away and heading toward the door. Sandy couldn't open it and leave though. She had to wait, her body visibly tense, for the man to unlock it.

Mr. Centerenian stared at Jane, his heavy brows lowered over his dark eyes. He studied her face and then the restraints. She sucked in a breath, afraid that he might test them. But finally he turned away, too, and unlocked the door by swiping his ID badge through a card-reading lock mechanism. The badge had his intimidating photograph on it, above his intimidating name.

Jane Doe was hardly intimidating. What the hell was her real name?

Once the door closed Jane was alone in the room,

and she struggled with her looser restraints. She tugged them up and down, working them against the railings of the bed, so that the fabric and Velcro loosened even more. But she weakened, too.

Panting for breath, she collapsed against the pillows piled on the raised bed and closed her eyes. Pain throbbed in her head, and she fought to focus. She needed to plan her escape.

Even if Jane got loose, she didn't have the ID badge she needed to get out of the room. But then how could she when she didn't even have an ID? Of course she was a patient here—not an employee.

But the slightly sympathetic nurse didn't have one, either. The only way Jane would get the hell out of this place was to get one of those card-reading badges off another employee.

The guard was armed, and Jane was too weak and probably too pregnant to overpower Mr. Centerenian anyway. So whatever employee or visitor stepped into her room next would be the one she ambushed.

Images flashed behind her closed eyes, images of her fists and feet flying—connecting with muscle and bone, as she fought for her life.

Against the guard?

Or were those brief flashes of memory of another time, another fight or fights?

Who the hell was Jane Doe really?

Chapter Two

A sigh of disappointment came from the man standing next to Aaron. "It's not Charlotte," he said.

The guy wasn't Whit Howell. Aaron had managed to leave him behind on St. Pierre Island. But this man had met him at the airport in Grand Rapids, Michigan. Once Aaron had dealt with his anger over the guy flagging his passport to monitor his travel, he had made use of him...for the fake credentials that had gotten Aaron on staff at Serenity House. Problem was that the U.S. Marshal had insisted on coming along.

Jason "Trigger" Herrema pushed his hand through his steel-gray hair. "Damn, I'd really hoped she was still alive."

"You and me both." The only difference was that Aaron wasn't entirely convinced that this woman wasn't Charlotte. Through the small window in the door of hospital room 00, he couldn't see much more than her perfect profile: slightly upturned nose, delicately sculpted cheekbone, heavily lashed eye.

Charlotte's partner didn't think it was her because Charlotte Green hadn't had a perfect profile...until she'd taken on the job of protecting the princess and had plastic surgery to make herself look exactly like the royal heiress. Because they had already shared the same build and coloring, it hadn't even taken much surgery to complete the transformation.

Aaron had seen a before photo of Charlotte; she'd had one of her and her aunt on the bedside table in her room in the palace in St. Pierre. She'd had a crooked nose from being broken too many times and an ugly, jagged scar on her cheek from a wanted killer's knife blade. It was no wonder her old partner didn't recognize her now.

But it had to be Charlotte.

Aaron couldn't look away from her; he couldn't focus on anyone but her, which was exactly how he had reacted the first time he'd met the tough female bodyguard. Even more than her beauty, he'd been drawn to her strength and her character. And even lying in that bed, she was strong—she had to be to have survived the attack in the hotel room in Paris.

"I need to talk to the princess," Aaron said. Obviously Charlotte hadn't told her old partner about her surgery, so neither would Aaron. If she had wanted the U.S. Marshal to know about her physical transformation, she would have informed him already. Maybe she hadn't trusted this guy. And if she hadn't, Aaron didn't dare trust him, either. "Someone needs to keep an eye out for the goon that was guarding her door."

They'd waited until the muscular man had slipped outside for a cigarette. "And maybe check around to see if Charlotte's been visiting her." He doubted it. If this was the princess and Charlotte knew she was here, she would have broken her out of this creepy hospital long ago.

Unless Charlotte wasn't who Aaron had thought she was. Unless she was the one keeping Gabriella here...

The Marshal nodded in agreement. "I can ask some of the nurses about her visitors and keep an eye out for the big guy."

"The princess knows me," Aaron said, "so I'll talk to her."

Trigger glanced inside the room again. "Just because she knows you doesn't mean you're going to get any information out of her."

"Maybe not," Aaron agreed. "But maybe she can shed some light on what happened in Paris—"

Trigger interrupted with an urgent whisper, "And what happened to Charlotte!"

"Exactly," Aaron said with a nod. "I have to try to find out what she knows."

Trigger's shoulders drooped in a shrug of defeat, as if he was already giving up. "Don't expect much. I doubt that girl knows anything. I worked with Charlotte for four years, and I never knew what was going on with her."

"I had a partner like that, too," Aaron muttered beneath his breath as the U.S. Marshal headed toward the nurses' station.

Was it possible that Whit had sold out? Was he the one behind what had happened in Paris?

And what about Charlotte? Had he been wrong about her, too? Maybe she'd had her own agenda where the princess was concerned.

Only one way to find out...

He clutched his fake ID badge and swiped it through the security lock beside the door. After a quick glance around to make sure no one was watching him, he slipped inside the room and shut the door at his back.

She didn't awaken; she didn't even stir in her sleep

or shift beneath the thick blankets covering her. Was she all right? Or heavily sedated?

If she was Charlotte, then whoever had brought her here would have had to keep her subdued somehow. Drugs made sense.

He stepped closer, checking for an IV, but there was nothing. However, her arms were strapped to the bed railings.

"Are you all right?" he whispered, reaching out to touch her. He tipped her face toward him. He'd been able to tell the women apart—because Gabriella was younger with a wide-eyed innocence. And because Charlotte had made his heart race. But now his heart slammed against his ribs when he noticed the angry bruise marring her silky skin. "Oh, my God...what the hell happened to you?"

This injury was not from the struggle in the hotel room. Much of the bruise was still brilliant with color; it was a recent wound.

Despite his hand cupping her face, she didn't react to his touch. Her lids didn't flicker; her thick lashes lay against her high cheekbones. He ran his fingertips along the edge of her jaw toward her throat to check for a pulse. But as he leaned over her, his arm brushed against her stomach and beneath the blanket, something shifted, almost as if kicking him.

It wasn't just her body beneath the heavy blankets. Or at least it wasn't the shape of her formerly lithely muscled body; it had changed due to the rounded mound of her stomach.

"Oh, my God!" He felt as if he had been kicked—and a hell of a lot harder than that slight movement against his arm.

This woman was pregnant. So she couldn't be Charlotte, who had been adamant about never becoming a mother. She had to be the princess. But he hadn't known…he hadn't realized…that the princess must have already been carrying a royal heir when she and Charlotte disappeared.

While he stared down at her stomach, she moved. Suddenly. Her hands wrapped tight around his throat, pushing hard against his windpipe. Despite the pressure he managed to gasp out one word, "Charlotte."

He had no doubt now—he had found *Charlotte*. And if her death grip was any indication, she wasn't happy that he had.

"CHARLOTTE…" she whispered the name back at him. It felt familiar on her lips. Was it her name? Or had she used it for someone else?

She wanted to ask the man, but for him to reply, she would have to loosen her grip. And then she wouldn't be able to overpower him. She'd caught him by surprise, playing possum as she had; otherwise she never would have managed to get her hands on him.

He was nearly as big as the other guard. But his body was all long, lean muscle. His hair was dark, nearly black, and his eyes were a startlingly light blue. His eyes struck a chord of familiarity within her just like the name he'd called her.

Did she know him? Or had she just seen him before in here? He had one of those name badges clipped to what was apparently a uniform shirt. It was a drab green that matched the drawstring pants of what looked like hospital scrubs. So he obviously worked here.

She needed that badge to escape. She needed to escape even more than she needed to know who the hell she was. But her grip loosened, as his hands grasped hers and easily pulled them from his throat. She cursed her weakness and then she cursed him. "You son of a bitch!" She wriggled, trying to tug her wrists from his grip. But his hands were strong. "Let me go!"

"I'm trying to help you," he said, his voice low and raspy—either from her attack or because he didn't want to be overheard.

"Then get me the hell out of here!"

"That's the plan."

Her breath shuddered out in a gasp of surprise. "It is?"

"It's why I'm here, Charlotte."

"Why—why do you think I'm Charlotte?" The question slipped out, unbidden. And now she silently cursed herself. If Charlotte was the woman he'd intended to free, then she should have let him believe she was Charlotte.

Hell, maybe she was.

His eyes, that eerily familiar pale blue, widened in surprise. "You're not?"

God, now he wasn't sure, either.

She should have kept her mouth shut, but maybe she had done that as long as she had physically been able. Her voice was raspy, as if she hadn't used it much lately. Or maybe someone had tried choking the life out of her, too.

She needed to get the hell out of this place. But should she leave with a stranger? Maybe he posed a bigger threat than the man with the Glock.

He studied her face, his gaze narrowing with the scrutiny. "Princess Gabriella?"

"Pr-princess?" she sputtered with a near-hysterical giggle. "You think I'm a princess?" Maybe it wasn't that ridiculous a thought, though. It was almost as if she had stumbled into some morbid fairy tale where the princess had been poisoned or cursed to an endless slumber.

Except she wasn't sleeping anymore.

"I don't know what the hell to think," the man admitted, shaking his head as if trying to sort through his confusion.

Maybe it wasn't the blow to her head that had knocked out her sense since he couldn't understand what was going on, either.

"Please," she urged him, "get me out of here." She glanced toward the window in the door, where the burly Mr. Centerenian usually stood guard. "Now."

"I need to know," he said. "Who are you? Gabby or Charlotte?"

Gabby? The name evoked the same familiar chord within her that Charlotte and his eyes had struck. It must have been a name she'd used. "Does it matter?" she asked. "Would you take one of us but leave the other?"

And why couldn't he tell the difference between the women? Was she a twin? Was there someone else, exactly like her, out there? Hurt? In danger? As freaking confused as she was?

He shook his head. "No, damn it, I wouldn't. You know I wouldn't leave either of you here."

Either of you...

Where was the other woman? Locked in another room in this hellhole? Jane's breath caught with fear and concern for a person she didn't even know. But then she didn't even know herself.

"But why won't you be honest with me?" the man asked, and hurt flashed in his pale blue eyes. "Don't you trust *me?*"

It was probably a mistake. But the admission slipped

out like her earlier question. "I don't even know who you are."

"Damn it, you have every right to be pissed, but it was the king's decision to make that announcement at the ball. He wouldn't listen to me…" he said then trailed off, and those pretty eyes narrowed again. "You're not talking about that. You're not just mad at me."

Maybe she was.

He definitely stirred up emotion inside her. Her pulse raced and her heart pounded hard and fast. Her mind didn't recognize him, but her body did as even her skin tingled in reaction to having touched his. An image flicked through her mind, of her hands sliding over his skin—all of his skin, his broad shoulders bare, his muscular chest covered only with dark, soft hair.

Then her fingers trailed down over washboard abs to…

Her head pounded as she tried to remember, but the tantalizing image slipped away as a ragged breath slipped between her lips. Despite the pounding, she shook her head and then flinched with pain and frustration. "No. I really don't know who you are."

He sucked in a sharp breath, as if her words had hurt him even more than her hands wrapped tightly around his throat had.

"Don't feel bad," she said with a snort of derision. "I don't know who I am, either."

"You don't?" His dark brows knitted together, furrowing his forehead. "You have amnesia?"

She jerked her head in a sharp nod, which caused her to wince in pain again. "I don't know who I am or why I'm here. But I know I'm in danger. I have to get the hell out of here."

Even if leaving with him might put her in more danger…

The door rattled. And she gasped. "You waited too long!"

While this man was probably stronger than the one who usually guarded her, this man was unarmed. He would be no more a match for the Glock than she had been.

The door creaked as it swung open. The man spun around, putting his body between hers and the intruder—as if using himself as a human shield.

"Timmer, we gotta go," a male voice whispered. "He's coming back."

A curse slipped from Timmer's lips. "We have to bring her with us."

"There's no time."

Anger flashed in those pale blue eyes. "We can't leave her here!"

"If we try to take her out, none of us will be able to leave."

The man—Timmer—nodded.

She grabbed him again, clutching at his arm. "Don't leave me!" she implored him.

"I'll be back," he promised.

"Hurry!" urged the other man, who hovered yet outside the room. "He's coming!"

Timmer turned back toward her, and taking her hand from his grasp, he quickly slipped her wrists back into the restraints and bound her to the bed.

He obviously hadn't intended to help her at all. Maybe it had all been a trick. Some silly game to amuse a bored guard…

As her brief flash of hope died, tears stung her eyes. But even in her physically weak state, she was too strong and too damned proud to give in to tears. She wouldn't cry. And she damn well wouldn't beg.

"I will come back," he said again, so sincerely that she was tempted to believe him.

But then he hurried from the room. Before the door swung completely shut behind him, she heard a shout. Voices raised in anger. Maybe even a shot.

She flinched at the noise, as if the bullet had struck her. As if they had sharp talons, fear and panic clutched at her heart. She was scared, and not just because if he were dead, he wouldn't come back and help her.

She was scared because she cared that he might be hurt, or even worse, that he might be dying. She'd had only a faint glint of recognition for him—for his unusually light eyes and for his skin…if that had been his body in that image that had flashed through her mind. However, she didn't remember his name or exactly how she'd known him.

She had known him very well; she was aware of that fact. Her stomach shifted as the baby inside her womb stirred restlessly, as if feeling her mother's fear and panic.

Or her *father's* pain?

AARON HAD STEPPED into it—right into the line of fire. The burly guard had caught him coming out of the room. The door hadn't even closed behind him yet, so he couldn't deny where he'd been—where he had been ordered never to go. Only a few employees were allowed into the room of the mysterious patient. Room 00.

Since he probably couldn't talk his way out of the situation, especially with the guy already reaching inside his suit jacket for his gun, Aaron tried getting the hell *out* of the situation. He ran away from the guard, in the direction that Trigger Herrema had already disappeared.

Some help the U.S. Marshal had proven to be…

With that guy as her partner, it was no wonder that Charlotte had left the U.S. Marshals and become a private bodyguard.

Was she now, despite her adamant resolve not to, about to become a mother? Or was that pregnant woman actually Princess Gabby?

He needed to know. But even more than that, he needed to get her the hell out of this place. He couldn't do either if he were dead.

Shouting echoed off the walls, erupting from the guard along with labored pants for breath. But he was either too far away, or the guy's accent too thick, for Aaron to make out any specific words. But he didn't need to know what the man said to figure out that it was a threat.

He skidded around corners of the hospital's winding corridors, staying just ahead of the lumbering guard. With a short breath of relief, he headed through the foyer to the glass doors of the exit. He would have to slow down to swipe his name badge through the card reader in order to get those doors to open.

But he never made it that far. Shots rang out. That was a threat he understood. He dropped to the ground. But he might have already been too late. Blood trickled down his face and dropped onto the white tiled floor beneath him.

He'd been hit.

Chapter Three

"You could have killed him," the woman chastised the guard, her voice a hiss of anger. "You could have killed other employees or patients. You were not supposed to use that gun. Again."

Through the crack the door had been left open, Aaron spied on the argument. Despite the man's superior height and burly build, he backed down from the woman. She was tall, too, with ash-blond hair pulled back into a tight bun. The plaque on her desk, which Aaron sat in front of, identified her as Dr. Mona Platt, the hospital administrator.

"That man is not an employee," the guard replied, his accent thick.

Aaron tried to place it. Greek? St. Pierre Island was close to Greece.

"He's a new hire," she replied, "who passed all the security clearances."

She had checked. She'd used her computer to pull up all of his fake information. He needed to know what other information was on her system, like the identity of the woman in Room 00. Or if not her identity, at least the identity of the person who had committed her to Serenity House.

Keeping an eye on the outer office where the two of them argued, Aaron moved around her desk and reached for her keyboard. He needed to pull up the financials. A place like this didn't accept patients for free. Someone had to be footing the bills.

Dr. Platt hadn't signed off her computer before leaving the room. And not enough time had passed since she'd left her desk that the screen had locked. He was able to access the employee records at which she'd been looking. But he needed *patient* records. However, he didn't know the patient's name. And if she was telling the truth, neither did the patient.

"He's not a nurse aide," the guard argued. "He could be a reporter."

"Not with those credentials," the administrator argued. "They're real. He passed our very stringent background check."

"Then he's not a reporter," the man agreed with a sigh of relief.

"That isn't necessarily a good thing," she warned him. "Since he had a legitimate reason for being here, he's more likely to go to the sheriff's office to report your shooting at him."

Aaron couldn't involve the authorities—couldn't draw any media or legal attention to the woman in Room 00. No matter who she was, it was likely to put her in more danger if her whereabouts became widely known.

"He can't go to the police if he can't leave," the man pointed out.

Aaron suppressed a shudder. Maybe instead of looking for information, he should have been looking for an escape. There was a window behind the desk, but like every other window in the place, it had bars behind the glass.

"We can't hold him here," she said. "Someone could report him missing, and we don't want the state police coming here asking questions. Or worse yet, with a search warrant."

"It is too dangerous to let him go," the man warned. "He could still go to the police."

"Yes, because you shot at him," she admonished him. "That was dangerous—for so many reasons!"

"I couldn't let him get away!" the man replied. "He was in *her* room."

"And she couldn't have told him anything," the administrator assured him. "*She* doesn't know anything to tell."

"But he must have recognized her..."

Aaron had but he still wasn't certain which woman she was. Her trying to strangle him had convinced him she was Charlotte. But part of Charlotte going above and beyond, besides plastic surgery, to protect the princess had been teaching the royal heiress how to protect herself. And Princess Gabby had never needed more protection than she did now.

So as not to draw their attention back to him, he lightly tapped the computer keyboard. But he wasn't certain what to enter. To pull up patient records, he needed the patient's name.

"All our employees sign a confidentiality agreement," the administrator reminded the guard. "He can't share what he saw with anyone without risking a lawsuit from Serenity House. Shooting at him was totally unnecessary."

"I still need to talk to him."

"You will only make the situation worse," she said. "If he does go to the authorities, I will be informed."

So she had a contact within the sheriff's office.

"Will you have enough warning for us to get her to a more secure location?"

"I don't know."

"You were paid handsomely to keep this location secure," the man said, his already gruff voice low with fury. "And since you have failed, I will handle this, and him, in my own way."

The guard wasn't going away. Instead of punching keys in the computer, Aaron needed to figure a way out of Serenity House—first for him and then for the patient in Room 00.

Room 00. He typed it in and the screen changed, an hourglass displaying while the computer pulled up records. He was almost in…

"What the hell are you doing?" the woman demanded to know as she slammed open the office door with such force it bounced off the wall and nearly struck her.

Aaron hit the exit key as he leaned across the keyboard, reaching for the box of tissues. He pulled one out and pressed it to his head. "I'm bleeding. That crazy son of a bitch was shooting at me."

He glanced behind her but the man was gone. Somehow she'd gotten rid of the goon—apparently with just a look as he'd overheard no words of dismissal. Maybe Aaron would have been in less danger if he'd gone with the guard because there was something kind of eerie about this steely-eyed woman.

"Yes, that was bad judgment on his part," she said, sounding nearly unconcerned about the shots now. "But maybe it wasn't uncalled for."

"Dr. Platt, I've done nothing to warrant an *execu-*

tion." He edged around her desk, toward the door. She blocked it, but as a trained bodyguard, he could easily overpower her—physically. Mentally, he didn't trust her—given the doctorate of psychology degree on her wall and her overall soulless demeanor.

"You entered a room that every employee," she said, "newly hired and long-term—has been warned is strictly off-limits."

He hadn't actually attended an orientation. But the guard posted at her door had certainly implied Room 00 was off-limits. "I thought I heard a yell for help. I was concerned—"

"Then you should have summoned the guard or the nurse who are authorized to enter that room. That is protocol," she stated, her voice cold with an icy anger. "By going inside yourself, you violated protocol."

"I wasn't thinking," he said. "I just reacted."

"You reacted incorrectly," she said. "And because of that, you can no longer be on staff at Serenity House." She held out her hand.

He moved to shake it, but she lifted her hand and ripped the ID badge from the lanyard around his neck. "You're fired, Mr. Ottenwess," she said, addressing him by the name on that ID badge.

"I would appreciate another chance," he said. "Now that I'm fully aware of the rules, I promise not to violate them again."

She shook her head. "That's a risk I can't take. And frankly, Mr. Ottenwess, staying here is a risk you can't take. I talked the private security guard out of interrogating you. But if he sees you again, I'm not sure what he might do to you."

Shoot at him again. And maybe the next time he wouldn't miss. The only thing that had nicked Aaron's cheek had been a shard of a porcelain vase that the guard had shot instead of him.

The burly guy had disappeared, but Aaron suspected he hadn't gone far. How could he get past him again to access Room 00?

"That's why I'm having my own guards escort you off the premises." As silently as she'd dismissed the private guard, she must have summoned her own because two men stood in the doorway.

"This isn't necessary," Aaron said. "I can show myself out."

"Actually you can't," she reminded him, "without your badge you can't open any of the facility doors—not to patients' rooms and not to exits. They will show you out." She barely lifted an ash-blond brow, but she had the two men rushing forward. Each guy grabbed one of his arms and dragged him from her office.

Aaron could have fought them off. They weren't armed. But he didn't want to beat them. He wanted to outsmart them. Or he had no hope of helping the woman in Room 00.

JANE HAD JUST resigned herself to the fact that the man, that the voice in the hall had addressed as *Timmer,* wasn't coming back…when the lock clicked and the door opened. She fought to keep her eyes closed and her breathing even, feigning sleep as she had when he'd entered the first time. Or at least the first time that she remembered.

"Is she really out?" the gruff-voiced guard asked someone.

Soft hands touched her face and gently forced open one of Jane's eyes. She stared up at the gray-haired nurse who dropped her lid and stepped back before replying, "She's unconscious."

"Did he hurt her?" Mr. Centerenian demanded to know.

"Who?" the nurse asked, her voice squeaking with anxiety. Over Jane or over lying to the guard?

"Someone was in her room," the man explained.

"He wouldn't have been able to talk her," Nurse Sandy easily lied again. She obviously hadn't been anxious about lying to him. "I gave her a sedative earlier, like you requested. She's completely out and oblivious to her surroundings."

Jane fought to keep her lips from twitching in reaction to the nurse's blatant lie. Wouldn't the guard remember that the nurse had given her no medication?

If only this woman had access to a door-opening name badge, Sandy could prove an even more valuable ally because Jane suspected she would help her escape if she could.

Of course the other man—*Timmer*—had promised he would return. Could he? Was he physically able to return?

"Good," the guard grunted. "And he won't get another chance to talk to her."

She held in a gasp as fear clutched her heart. Had one of those shots struck the man?

"Why—why won't he?" the nurse nervously asked the question burning in Jane's mind.

The guard did not answer, just issued another order. "Leave now."

"But—but I should stay to monitor her—"

"Leave now," Mr. Centerenian repeated.

The lock clicked again and the door opened with a creak of hinges and rush of cool air from the hall. It closed again, shutting in the stale air that smelled faintly of the cigarette smoke that always clung to the guard.

Had Mr. Centerenian left with Nurse Sandy? Was Jane alone again?

She nearly opened her eyes but then the guard spoke again. Since the older woman had left, he wasn't talking to the nurse.

Jane peered through a slit in one lid and saw that his cell phone was pressed to his ear. He spoke in a language she couldn't place but somehow understood. She interpreted his side of the conversation.

"There is a problem," he said. "Someone got inside her room tonight. He saw her…"

Mr. Centerenian grunted in response to whatever the person he called told him and then agreed, "Yes, it is no longer safe to keep her here. I will bring her and your unborn child to the airport tomorrow night to meet your private plane."

Who the hell was the guard talking to? Who was the father of her unborn child? She had suspected it was the man who'd snuck into her room. If not him, then who?

She barely restrained her urge to attack the guard and demand that he tell her who he was talking to, who he was bringing her to meet. But she couldn't risk getting hit again. An apparent blow had already cost her too much—of her strength and her mind.

And she needed all she had of both to escape before the guard brought her to the airport. She feared that if she got on that private plane, that she would have no hope of ever regaining her freedom.

She couldn't trust that the man who had snuck in would keep his word to return and help her. She didn't know if he even could—if Timmer had survived his confrontation with the guard. She waited but Mr. Centerenian said nothing of the man he'd caught in her room.

Was he alive or dead?

And who the hell was he or *had* he been to her?

PAIN EXPLODED IN Aaron's stomach, sending his breath from his lungs in a whoosh. He doubled over, hanging from the arms holding him back. Not that he couldn't have broken free had he wanted to fight. But as he writhed around in an exaggerated display of pain, he lurched forward and *accidentally* fell against the guard who was using him as a punching bag.

"And don't come back unless you want more of that," the man warned as he pushed Aaron back. He pushed him through the gate he'd already opened that led from the building to the employee parking lot.

The lot was behind the big brick building and dimly lit. The few parking lights flickered and cast only a faint glow that reflected off the windshields and metal of the cars filling the lot. Darkness was gathering, pushing the last traces of daylight into night.

The gate snapped shut behind him and the lock buzzed. That gate and the one between the guest parking lot and front entrance were the only ways through the sixteen-foot-high fence surrounding the building.

Serenity House was a freaking fortress—more prison than hospital. If Charlotte was the woman in Room 00, it was no wonder that she hadn't managed to escape yet—despite her skills. Of course if she'd been telling him the truth, she'd forgotten all those skills…except for how to strangle him. Only she hadn't been as strong as the woman he remembered—as the woman with whom he'd made love one unforgettable night.

Images flashed through his mind. Moonlight caressing honey-toned skin and sleek curves. His hands following the path of the moonlight. Then his lips…

And her hands and her soft lips, touching him everywhere. Passionate kisses, bodies entwined…

His breath shuddered out in a ragged sigh as he shook off those skin-tingling memories. That had been one incredible night. And even though they'd used protection, it wasn't foolproof.

Was that baby she carried his? The dates would probably be about right. But was the woman?

He would find out soon. For the sake of the guards who watched him yet from behind the gate, he stumbled across the parking lot with the drunkenlike stagger of a boxer who'd taken too many hits.

Aaron had driven separately from the U.S. Marshal, which was good since Jason "Trigger" Herrema had left him without a backward glance. Some partner Trigger must have been to Charlotte. No wonder she was so strong and independent. And no wonder she had resigned from the U.S. Marshals for private security.

But Charlotte Green wasn't the only one with skills. Aaron clutched the ID badge he had lifted from the guard who'd hit him. The guy had seemed too arrogant an SOB to admit or even realize that Aaron had taken the badge off him. At least not right away. But he might eventually figure it out. So Aaron had to act quickly.

But not too quickly that they were waiting and ready for him to try something. He also needed backup. Obviously he couldn't count on Trigger, the man, so he needed another kind of trigger—one on a gun.

He hurried toward his vehicle, which was a plain gray box of a sedan that he'd rented at the airport. His gun wasn't inside but back at the cottage he'd found in the woods near Serenity House. He hadn't rented it; he hadn't needed to—it had looked abandoned or at least out of season for the owners. The cottage was close enough that he'd figured they would be able to run there if they weren't able to reach his vehicle.

But now that he had seen Charlotte or Princess Gabriella or whoever the hell she was and realized how weak she was, he suspected that outrunning anyone was out of the question.

He needed wheels and a very powerful engine. Maybe he should have gone for fast rather than nondescript when he'd rented a car. Just as he was considering his choice, shots rang out—shattering the rear window. He ducked down, easing around the trunk toward the driver's side. Maybe if he kept the car between him and Serenity House, the guards wouldn't have a clear shot—if they were the ones shooting. But he'd seen no weapons on them. Then the driver's side windows shattered, bullets striking first the rear window and then the front window.

"I'm not getting the deposit back on this rental," he murmured as he clicked the key fob to unlock the doors. He could have just reached through the shattered window and unlocked it himself, but he didn't want to raise his head too high for fear that it might be the next thing a bullet hit.

He didn't even know where the hell the shots were coming from. Serenity House? Or somewhere in the parking lot behind him?

He ducked down farther, suspecting the shots might have been coming from behind him. Maybe he had his answer about where the hell the private security guard had gone. Instead of standing sentry outside Room 00, he'd set up an ambush outside Serenity House.

With the door unprotected, Aaron had the best

chance to free Charlotte or Princess Gabriella. But he couldn't go back inside. Shots kept firing, and he knew it was just a matter of time before one struck him. He had to get the hell out of here while he still could.

Chapter Four

Shots rang out, echoing inside Jane's aching head. She reached for her gun, but it wasn't on the holster. Hell, she wasn't even wearing the holster. Instead her fingers encountered the soft mound of her burgeoning belly. Of her baby…

She jolted awake, as if fighting her way out of a nightmare. But she awakened *to* the nightmare, not *from* it. She still couldn't remember who she was or how she had wound up trapped in this strange hospital jail. But she hadn't forgotten that she needed to get the hell out of here.

And not to that private airport. She couldn't let the surly Mr. Centerenian take her there. When? Tomorrow night? Tonight? She had no idea how long she'd been asleep. She wore no watch, and there was no clock for her to mark the seconds, minutes or hours.

Given the urgency of her situation, how had she fallen asleep? Was she the one to whom the nurse had really lied? Had Sandy actually slipped her a sedative? But Jane didn't feel groggy from drugs. She was just tired—either because of the concussion or the pregnancy.

The baby shifted inside her, kicking against her ribs

as if trying to prod her into action—reminding Jane that she had someone besides herself to protect now. No matter who the father was—*she* was the mother. Something primal reared up inside her, clutching at her heart and her womb. A mother's instinct, a mother's love. This was *her* child.

Her baby girl. She felt it with a deep certainty that the baby she carried was a girl. Had she had an ultrasound? Even though she didn't remember the process, maybe she remembered the results.

"Okay, baby girl, I don't know how we got here," she murmured. "But that doesn't matter right now. What matters is that we're getting out."

She just had to figure out how. She tugged on her wrists, fighting to loosen the restraints. Maybe that man—Mr. Timmer—hadn't tightened them as much as she'd feared. Or maybe the nurse had returned and loosened them while Jane had been sleeping. Either way, she had enough play to slip one hand free. Just as she reached out to undo the other strap, the lock beeped. And hinges creaked as the door opened.

Damn it! Maybe she had slept too long. Maybe she'd slept away a day and any chance she'd had of escaping this nightmare of captivity.

SHE WAS STILL HERE.

Aaron's breath shuddered out with a sigh of relief. He had worried that they might have moved her already, that they probably had just minutes after he'd been discovered in her room. But then maybe they didn't realize those last shots—fired at him in the parking lot—had also missed him.

As he studied her, his relief ebbed away, and his concern returned. She lay, her body stiff and unmoving beneath her blankets. Maybe when they hadn't managed to get rid of him, they'd decided to get rid of her instead. Was she dead? Or just playing dead like she had the first time he had come into her room?

He moved toward the bed, hoping that she would reach out to strangle him as she had last time. She wasn't strong enough to hurt him but it proved she was still strong enough to fight.

He opened his mouth to whisper her name but had no idea what to call her. Was she Charlotte or Princess Gabriella? He wished he knew. Since he wished she was the woman he had already begun to fall for, he called her, "Charlotte…"

Her eyes opened wide with shock, but probably at the sound of his voice rather than any recognition of her name because she said, "I thought you were dead."

"So did I," Aaron admitted.

If the Marshal hadn't shown up in the parking lot when he had, those shots probably wouldn't have stopped until Aaron had been hit. And killed. But Marshal Herrema's car pulling into the lot had sent the shooter into hiding. Aaron suspected he would come out again—just hopefully not until Aaron got *her* to safety.

"We have to get out of here," he said, reaching for her restraints.

But she already had one arm free and quickly freed her other arm. "I thought you were shot," she said. "I was sure I heard gunshots."

"You did," he confirmed.

"The guard with the Glock?" She swung her legs over the bed but hesitated to stand.

"Yes." She knew guns. She had to be Charlotte, or had Charlotte taught Princess Gabriella to identify firearms? "He caught me coming out of your room."

She glanced toward the door, her caramel-colored eyes widening with fear. "After catching you, I'm surprised he would leave my side for a second—even for his nicotine fix."

Her fear made him think she was the princess. Because he'd never seen fear on Charlotte's face. Passion. Anger. But the fear had been Gabriella's.

"I came up with a distraction to get him away." Trigger, in a short dark-haired wig that made him, from a distance, look like Aaron. "But we don't have much time." Before the guard either gave up trying to catch Trigger or caught him and figured out he wasn't Aaron.

She gestured at her hospital gown. "I won't be able to just walk out of here dressed like this, and I don't think I have anything else to wear. There's no bureau or closet in here."

He'd noticed that the first time he had broken into the room. There had been no sign of her belongings—nothing to provide a clue to her identity or a wardrobe for her departure. So he had come prepared. He handed her the wad of clothes he'd had clenched under his arm. She unfolded the drab green shirt and pants. He'd stolen the scrubs from the employee locker room. He reached for her arm to guide her from the bed, so that she could change.

She stood but swayed on her bare feet.

Aaron grabbed her. "Are you all right?"

The blow to her head had obviously stolen more than her memory. Would he be able to get her out without assistance? Maybe he should have brought along a wheelchair.

She drew in a deep breath and, using his arm, steadied herself. "I'm fine."

"Do you need help getting out of the gown?" he

asked. And images flashed through his mind of another time he'd undressed her...

"No. I can manage myself." She hadn't lost her stubborn independence. She had to be Charlotte.

"Turn around," she ordered him, her modesty misplaced. If she was Charlotte, he had already seen every inch of her naked. He had already caressed and kissed every inch of her naked skin.

But he obliged her and turned back toward the door and kept watch through the small window to the hall. For a big building—three stories of brick and mortar—the place was surprisingly quiet and nearly deserted. Where were all the other patients and visitors? Locked up and locked out?

"Actually I can't manage," she corrected herself. "These damn ties are knotted in the back. Can you undo them?"

He drew in a deep breath to steady his suddenly racing pulse, and then he turned to face her again. She stood with her back toward him, her long hair pulled over her shoulder so it would be out of the way. She had already pulled on the pants and stepped into the slip-on shoes. Her arm over her shoulder, she contorted as she tugged on the straps binding her inside the hospital gown.

"You're making it worse," he observed and gently pulled away her fingers. Forcing his fingers to remain steady, he unknotted the ties and parted the rough cotton fabric.

Baring her back reminded him of lowering the zipper on another kind of gown—one of whisper-soft silk that had slid down her body like a caress—leaving her bare but for a tiny scrap of lace riding low on her hips. She wore no bra now, either. Maybe she thought turning away from him protected her modesty. But he could see the side of her full breast and the nipple puckered with cold. But the rounded mound of her belly drew his attention from the beauty of her breast.

This was another kind of beauty.

One that stole away his breath. Was the baby she carried his? That was only possible if she was Charlotte. While he suspected that she was, he wasn't certain if that was merely wishful thinking on his part rather than fact. Hell, not even she knew for certain who the hell she was—if he could believe her claim of amnesia.

She tugged the scrubs shirt down over her breasts and burgeoning belly. The cotton stretched taut. He should have found her a bigger size, but he'd grabbed what he could from the first accessible locker. He'd acted quickly then because they didn't have much time.

"Are you ready?" he asked, the urgency rushing back over him. Trigger might have already been caught. Time was running out. "Do you have everything?"

"There's nothing here," she said. "We shouldn't be here, either." As she turned toward him, she swayed again and clutched at his arm.

"You're not fine," he said, disproving her earlier claim. "You're weak and dizzy."

"I will be fine," she amended herself. "Once we get out of here. Let's go." And then instead of holding on to his arm for support, she was tugging on it to pull him toward the door. "You still have your badge?"

He shook his head even as he pulled the ID from the lanyard around his neck. "Not mine."

This was probably better. Since it belonged to one of the Serenity House security guards, it had access to more areas than Mr. Ottenwess's badge had.

"I was fired."

"Then how did you get back in?" she asked, her golden-brown eyes narrowing with suspicion.

He lifted the badge toward the lock. "I grabbed this off the guy throwing me off the premises." His stomach clenched in protest of the blows it had taken to provide the distraction. He could have fended those off and would have had he not needed that damn badge.

Her brow furrowed now—with suspicion. "Who are you?"

He sucked in a breath of disappointment. "You still don't remember me?"

"I don't remember anything before I woke up in this place." But she looked away from him as she said it, as if unable to meet his eyes.

Why? Because she lied? But why lie about having amnesia? Was she playing him for a fool?

What the hell was going on? Was this whole disappearance just a way to get the princess out of the obligation the king had announced at the ball? That was what Rafael St. Pierre and Whit had suspected until they'd seen the hotel suite.

But Aaron had believed Charlotte too honest for subterfuge. Had he been wrong about her?

It wouldn't be the first time he had let his attraction to a woman cloud his judgment. The last time his lapse had cost that woman her life.

He had to be more careful—had to make certain that nobody died this time. Because, given all the bullets that had already been fired at him, it just might be him who wound up dead this time.

JANE HELD HER breath as she waited for him to swipe the badge he'd stolen through the lock. But he hesitated, his gaze fixated on her. Even though she wasn't looking at him, she knew those pale blue eyes were staring at her. He wasn't touching her, but yet she *felt* him. Her skin heated and tingled as it had from just the brush of his fingertips as he'd untied her gown.

She closed her eyes and drew in a steadying breath. But that was a mistake because that fleeting image she'd had earlier of him returned—even more vividly. She not only felt him. She *saw* him. Naked.

Her face heated with embarrassment over that being the only thing she remembered about her life before she had woken up in this place. That was why she'd lied to him. How could she admit to knowing what he looked like naked—*magnificent*—but not what his name was?

She'd only heard that voice from the hall refer to him as Timmer. But she didn't even know if that was really his name or a cover he'd used to gain access to this creepy place.

Hell, she didn't even know what *her* name was.

But none of that mattered right now.

"We have to get out of here," she urged him. "Mr. Centerenian, that armed guard, called someone—I don't know who—earlier, and they made plans to take me to some airfield—to get me out of the country." She had no idea what country they were in, but that didn't matter, either. What mattered was not getting on that private plane to a new prison.

He nodded, either in understanding of the guard's plan or in agreement with the need to get out of here because he swiped the badge through the card reader.

She held her breath until the lock buzzed and a green light flashed on the card reader. She reached for the door, but his hand was already on the handle. Her fingers connected with the back of his hand, with his hard knuckles and warm skin. And she tingled again from his touch, just as she had when he'd undressed her. Attraction had chased chills up and down her spine then. Now apprehension did as he opened the door to the hall.

Would the guard catch them as he'd caught this man last time?

Now that Timmer had unlocked the door, he was done hesitating. His hand wrapped tight around her arm. Maybe just to steady her. Or maybe to make sure that she didn't get away from him.

He pulled her down the hall behind him, as if keeping himself between her and whatever threat they might encounter. As she followed him, she noticed the bulge beneath the scrubs at the small of his back. He wasn't unarmed this time. Since she'd seen him last, Timmer had acquired a gun. Was it his or had he taken it off the burly guard?

Was that where Mr. Centerenian had gone? Disarmed? Or dead?

Maybe this man, whom she'd once known intimately, was just resourceful. Or maybe he was dangerous.

The threat actually came from behind them as someone yelled, "Stop!"

The man increased his speed, nearly dragging her as Jane obeyed the command and tried to stop. It wasn't a male voice yelling but a familiar female voice. Nurse Sandy caught up to them and clutched at Jane's free arm.

"Stop!" But the older woman spoke to the man. "You can't take her."

"I can't stay," Jane told her. "That guard—the one who hurt me—he's going to take me out of here. Out of the country. I can't leave with him."

"You can't leave with this man, either," the nurse

said. "Unless…" Sandy stared intently into Jane's eyes. "Do you know him?"

"I—I—"

"Of course you don't," the woman answered her own question. "You don't even know who you are."

"Tell me," Jane implored the nurse. "You know. Tell me!"

She shook her head. "I can't. And I can't let you leave." She held on tightly to Jane's arm as the man tugged on her other arm.

Feeling like the rope, pulled taut to the point of fraying, in a game of tug-of-war, Jane summoned all her strength and wrestled free of both of them. "I have to get out of here!"

"Don't leave with him," the woman implored again. "You don't know him."

As if the adrenaline coursing through Jane had awakened the baby, she shifted inside her womb. Or maybe she was trying to send her mother a message. "I think I knew him—that I would know him if I had my memory."

"That doesn't mean you should trust him," the nurse said. "If he was on the up-and-up, he would have come here with the police—not all by himself."

"I didn't come alone," the man replied. There had been the other one in the hall, warning Timmer to leave before the guard came back. "I brought a U.S. Marshal with me."

At the mention of a Marshal, Jane shivered—her blood chilling. Who the hell was the Marshal? And how would she know one? Was she a wanted criminal?

"You don't have a warrant or any legal reason to take her," the nurse said with absolute certainty.

"There's no time to get before a judge and get one," he replied.

"There isn't," Jane agreed. The guard had already made plans to take her away. This man wouldn't have had time to obtain a warrant.

And then whatever time they had had ran out because someone else shouted. The burly guard lumbered toward them. Mr. Centerenian wasn't alone—two other, slighter men followed close behind him. When they caught sight of Jane with Timmer, they surpassed the guard.

As he had before, Timmer stepped between Jane and the threat—bracing himself as if to take a blow. But he dodged the fist thrown at him and instead threw one of his own with such force that he dropped his would-be assaulter to the ground.

The guy grunted and clutched his head while his co-worker stepped over him, his arms already swinging. Jane's protector braced himself with a wide stance, but instead of throwing another punch, he kicked out. His foot connected with the man's jaw, sending him backward over the guard already sprawled on the ground.

Who the hell was Timmer? What kind of experience had equipped him to break in and out of secure facilities and beat up men nearly as big as he was?

But before Jane could ask him any questions, the guard usually posted outside her door lifted his weapon and stared down the barrel at him. Mr. Centerenian wouldn't shoot her—not when he had plans to take her away.

His intent was clear. He was going to kill the man who had tried to help her escape. And if he succeeded, her chances of ever regaining her freedom would be dead, as well. But she cared less about getting away than she cared about Timmer. No matter who or what he was—he had mattered to her.

Chapter Five

Aaron reached for his gun, but he was too late. Metal scraped his spine as someone pulled the weapon from the waistband of his drawstring pants. He'd been so focused on the guards rushing him that he'd forgotten about the nurse. But it wasn't her. The older woman had flattened herself against the corridor wall to avoid the fight and the bullets that would inevitably fly.

The barrel of the guard's gun pointed right at Aaron's face—his own gun probably pointed at the back of his head. Either way, this wasn't going to end well for him.

A shot rang out, reverberating off the walls. He flinched at the noise and in anticipation of the pain. But he wasn't the one who cried out with it. The burly guard uttered a foreign curse as he dropped his gun from his bleeding hand. One of the Serenity House guards reached for the discarded weapon, but another shot rang out. And another curse as blood spurted from torn knuckles.

"What the hell!"

Aaron repeated the sentiment. "What the hell—" He whirled toward the shooter who stood beside him. Recognition and relief clutched his heart, squeezing it tight in his chest.

Charlotte.

"Let's go," she said as she backed quickly down the hall.

He shook his head at her and then addressed the guards. "Toss your ID badges over here."

Their eyes hard with rage and hatred, they just stared up at him.

Another shot rang out and Charlotte gestured at them with the gun. "Do as he says or the next bullet I fire will do some serious damage!"

They tugged off their badges—the two who still had theirs—and tossed them onto the floor.

"You, too," she warned the other.

"I don't have it!" the man exclaimed, casting a vicious glare at Aaron.

Charlotte's lips curved into a small smile. "You took his?"

Aaron nodded. He leaned over and grabbed up the badges and the gun.

"Now let's go," she said.

He wanted to, but he couldn't leave yet. Trigger might have taken off on him earlier, but he had returned. "Where's the Marshal?" he asked the first guard she'd shot—the man who wore the suit instead of hospital scrubs.

The man was still cursing beneath his breath while he clutched at his bleeding hand. "Who?"

"We have to get out of here," Charlotte urged him. Clutching his arm with her free hand, she tugged impatiently.

"The Marshal," Aaron repeated. It wasn't the only question he wanted to ask the man; he wanted to know who the hell he was working for, too. But first he had to know if the Marshal was all right. "The man wearing the wig to look like me—where is he?"

The guard shrugged. "He's gone..."

"We should be gone, too," Charlotte said.

She was right. More guards or the police could have been called and were already on their way. His other questions and answers would have to wait until he got Charlotte safely out of Serenity House.

Aaron agreed with her—with action. Keeping an eye on the guards to make sure no one followed them, he steered her through the lobby to the exit doors. A quick swipe of his badge had the doors sliding open, but then an alarm blared. The noise was louder even than the shots that she had fired, causing him to flinch and for his heart to slam into his ribs.

The doors stopped and began to close. Aaron gently pushed Charlotte through the narrowing gap. Then he turned sideways and tried to squeeze through behind her. The metal edges of the glass doors scraped against his hip and shoulder, threatening to crush him as the doors continued to close. But he made it through the narrow space just before it closed completely.

Alarms sounded outside, too. Aaron swiped his badge through the card reader in the gate, but the red light kept blinking. And the alarms kept blaring.

Charlotte squinted and grimaced—probably in more pain from the bruise on her head than in fear. She'd been almost too weak to stand up back in her room. The physical exertion might be too much for her. But before Aaron could reach for her, she lifted her gun toward the lock and fired at it—in sheer frustration and anger. Sparks ignited from the machine, glinting off the metal. "It won't open."

Not now. He couldn't even try another badge since

the reader caught fire. And there was no way he could get Charlotte over the gate—not with the men rushing through the lobby behind them.

He glanced through the fence, to where a car idled in the front lot. "Stand back!" he shouted at her, as the engine revved.

Tires screeched as the car headed right toward the gate. And them.

JANE LIFTED HER gun and aimed it at the windshield. It was already broken, the glass shattered. She couldn't get a clear target, only the vague shadow of a man behind the wheel. This shot might not be as nonlife-threatening as the other shots she had fired. But before she could squeeze the trigger, a hand closed over hers and shoved down the gun.

"Don't shoot!"

The car kept coming, right at them. She struggled to lift her arm, but her strength wasn't back yet. She couldn't overpower a man like this—one so strong he'd easily fought off two men. Timmer's arms closed around her, lifting her off her feet. Her legs flailed, but she didn't kick at him. He was already moving, carrying her away from the fence.

Metal crunched as the car careened through the gate, crumpling it and the fence around it. She screamed—more with frustration than fear. Would she ever be able to escape?

Then the man changed direction, carrying her toward the car instead of away from it. Timmer opened the passenger's side rear door and pushed her inside, onto the backseat. Had the nurse been right? Had Jane been a fool to trust a man she didn't know, or at least that she couldn't remember?

Before he could climb in beside her, the guards reached him—tugging him from the car as it backed away from the building. The gate tangled beneath it, sparks flying as the car dragged it across the asphalt.

"Stop!" she screamed at the driver. "Don't leave him!" Her mind couldn't recall more than how he looked naked, but her heart—which beat frantically with panic—remembered him. Had she loved him? And if she had, how could she have forgotten him?

And if the man behind the wheel was the partner of the other man, why wasn't he helping him? Instead he glanced into the rearview mirror and studied her. "Charlotte?"

It felt more familiar—more right—than it even had the first time that Timmer had called her that name. But was it hers?

She remembered the weapon clenched in her hand and lifted it again, training it at the back of the man's head, she told him again, "Stop!"

"Charlotte," he repeated with the same certainty she had heard from Timmer when she'd tried to strangle him.

She cared less about who she was than his safety right now, though. Ignoring the driver even while she kept her gun trained on him, she turned back to the fight going on inside the gate. The man didn't need her help this time. Hell, he wouldn't have last time if she hadn't pulled his weapon before he'd had the chance.

He had the guard's gun, but he used his feet and fists, knocking down the guards as easily as he had inside the building. Then he ran toward the car, jumping inside the door she'd left open for him.

"She's Charlotte," the driver told him, turning from behind the wheel to look at his backseat passengers.

"How the hell is she Charlotte looking like that—looking exactly like Princess Gabriella?"

"Get out of here!" Timmer ordered him, pointing toward the guards rushing toward them.

As the car backed away, a tall woman ran out of the building. It wasn't the nurse but another woman, one who shouted with an anger that was more intense than Mr. Centerenian's. Her shouts were clearly audible through the broken windows. Had every window of the car been shot out? When?

The woman yelled, "Don't let them get away!"

Jane shivered.

Timmer pulled the door shut and wrapped an arm around her shoulders. "Are you all right?"

"Not yet," she murmured. "Not until we're far away from this place."

But they didn't go far—just a few sharp turns on dark back roads and the car pulled up in front of a cottage. Headlights glinted off dark windows. The place looked abandoned.

"Where are we?" she asked. "Are we still on the grounds of that horrible place?" She shuddered at the thought. She wanted—she *needed*—to be much farther away.

"They'll be checking airports and train stations," Timmer replied as he opened the back door again and stepped onto the driveway, gravel crunched beneath his shoes. He held out his hand for her. "This'll give us some time…"

"Time for you to explain what you're up to this time, Charlotte," the driver said, his voice gruff with bitterness. He reached over the seat and caught her arm before she could slide out.

Her fingers were grasped in the other man's hand—

leaving her feeling again like that rope in a demented game of tug-of-war. And that rope was getting even more frayed as exhaustion overwhelmed her.

"You're not going anywhere until you tell me what I want to know," the driver said. With his free hand he dragged off a dark wig, revealing coarse-looking iron-gray hair.

The man was threatening despite or maybe because of the fact that he seemed vaguely familiar. She may have known him before but definitely not as intimately as she had known the younger man. And she had certainly never trusted this man.

It was nothing—*what she remembered*—so damn little that it made her laugh. She wasn't all that different from the baby she carried—starting out all over again—with no past.

At least no past that she could clearly recall…

"You think this is funny?" the man asked, a vein beginning to bulge in his forehead with frustration that she wasn't taking him seriously.

No. But now that she had started laughing, she couldn't stop. It was all so ridiculous—how could she have forgotten *everything?*

"What's so damn funny?" he demanded to know, his voice sharp with anger.

She gasped for breath and tears rolled down her face. But she couldn't stop.

"What's wrong with her?" the driver asked the other man.

"She doesn't remember anything, Trigger."

Like his roughly lined face, the name struck a chord with Jane. A very unpleasant chord that had her breath catching in her throat.

"What do you mean?" Trigger asked. "You don't even know what I was going to ask her."

"The only thing you should be asking her about is what happened in Paris or where she's been the past six months." Timmer's light blue eyes narrowed with suspicion. "Unless you're here for some other reason than breaking her out of that psychiatric hospital?"

Paris? Six months lost? Timmer had also mentioned some things earlier—about princesses and kings and announcements. Jane wanted to know about those things and so much more. But she didn't want to talk in front of this man—this guy named Trigger. She tugged on her arm, but he held tightly to her yet, refusing to release her.

"I—uh," he stammered, "there is some other information I need from Charlotte."

Timmer tugged on her other arm, trying to pull her free of the driver. "She's not Charlotte."

"I know she doesn't look exactly like her," Trigger said. "But her voice…"

Timmer chuckled. "The princess is so adept at learning languages that she picks up the dialects of the people she spends the most time with. So of course she picked up her American accent from Charlotte and sounds just like her."

So there was another woman out there that not only looked like her but sounded like her, too?

Trigger shook his head, obviously still unwilling to accept Timmer's explanations. "But the way she holds a gun…"

"Charlotte taught her how to shoot. She taught her how to defend herself."

So despite the certainty with which Timmer had said her name, he wasn't really sure who she was. Or at least he now appeared positive that she was the princess when earlier he'd seemed convinced she was Charlotte. Until Jane reclaimed her memory—and all of her memories—she had no idea which of these two women she actually was.

"Since they were that close," Trigger persisted, "maybe Charlotte talked to her about some of our old cases."

Timmer groaned in obvious frustration with the other man's stubbornness. "You yourself said that Charlotte kept everything to herself. You doubted the princess would know anything."

Jane dragged in a deep breath as her own frustration overwhelmed her. "I don't know *anything*. I don't even know who I am."

The guy studied her face intently. "Then it's possible she's Charlotte and that Charlotte had a nose job and that scar fixed…"

Jane wanted to reach a hand up to her nose and her cheek. But she couldn't move her hands. She was trapped, her arms bound as effectively as the restraints had tied her up and made her helpless.

But Jane wasn't helpless. While her memory was gone, her common sense was not. She moaned and sagged against the seat, faking a faint.

AARON'S HEART SLAMMED against his ribs as he watched her go limp. He reached inside the car and caught the woman up in his arms, tugging her free of Trigger's grasp. Careful to not hit her head against the roof, he lifted her through the door and carried her toward the house. She was light but she wasn't limp. Her body was still tense. With fear? Was she so frightened that she couldn't relax even in unconsciousness?

Her actions back at Serenity House hadn't been fearful. More fearless.

But maybe the fight she'd put up had exhausted her to the point of passing out. He needed to get her inside. He needed to get her away from Trigger.

The car headlamps illuminated the entrance to the tiny clapboard and fieldstone house. Aaron didn't bother searching for a hidden key to the front door, and he didn't waste time walking around to the back door that he'd unlocked earlier that evening. Instead he lifted her higher in his arms and kicked open the front door.

"I could've gotten that for you," Trigger said, as he hurried inside after them. He pulled a sheet from a couch and stood there, waiting for Aaron to lay her down.

Aaron didn't want the U.S. Marshal anywhere near her, so he held her yet in his arms. "Why did you really flag my passport?" he asked. "What was your real reason for wanting to find Charlotte?"

"You called *me*," Trigger reminded him. "You wanted *my* help to find her."

Because he'd thought that if she was in trouble—or hiding the princess from her controlling father—that she would have reached out to friends. It was only now that he realized she and Trigger may have been partners, but they had probably never been friends.

Not like he and Whit had once been friends. But that seemed like a lifetime ago now.

"I know why I called you," Aaron said. "But why did you agree to help find her? What information did you want from her?"

Instead of answering Aaron's question, Trigger asked one of his own. "You really don't think she's Charlotte?"

Aaron finally settled her onto the couch. The headlamps shining through the open door illuminated her flawlessly beautiful face. "Look at her. *Really* look at her. What do you think?"

"She's been missing for almost six months. She could have had plastic surgery," Trigger said, stubbornly clinging to that possibility.

She'd actually had the surgery long before she'd disappeared, but Aaron felt compelled to continue lying to the Marshal. "Is Charlotte the kind of woman who would ever get plastic surgery?"

"What I knew of Charlotte, no," Trigger admitted. "The woman had no vanity. She cared about nothing but keeping people safe. And because of that, she might have had it, so she could protect the princess."

Charlotte's former partner knew her better than he thought he had.

But then Marshal Herrema shook his head. "That would be extreme, though, even for Charlotte. But even if it's Princess Gabriella, she might know something. Maybe Charlotte talked about…"

"About what?" Aaron asked. "What do you want to know about?"

Trigger shrugged. "An old case."

"If it's old, why does it matter now?"

"The witness is missing."

"Just now?" Could that case have had something to do with what had happened in Paris? Had someone gone after Charlotte to find out where the witness was?

Trigger sighed. "The witness has actually been missing for a while, and it's important we find her."

If she'd been missing before Charlotte disappeared, wouldn't he have already contacted her? And if Charlotte hadn't told him then, she must have had her reasons for keeping the witness's location secret from her former partner.

"Charlotte left the Marshals a few years ago," Aaron recalled. "How would she know anything about where this witness is now?"

"They got close."

Like she and Princess Gabby had.

"If anyone knows where she is, Charlotte does," Trigger said.

Aaron gestured at the unconscious woman on the couch. "That's not Charlotte," he lied. At least he was pretty damn certain he was lying.

"But since that woman was her friend, Charlotte might have talked about her. Or maybe the princess overheard Charlotte talking to the witness…"

"It wouldn't matter if she had," Aaron said. "She has amnesia. She doesn't remember anything now."

"Not even you?"

He shook his head. "No. She may never get her memory back." That was another lie because he was determined for her to remember. Him.

"Amnesia is her excuse for forgetting," Aaron continued. "What's yours?"

"What?"

"We had a plan," he reminded the Marshal. "After we got her out, you were going to go to the police and have them get a warrant to seize Serenity House records to find out who the hell put her in that place."

Trigger stared at the sleeping woman for another minute, as if he was having an inner debate about whether or not she was Charlotte. Aaron recognized the look since he'd been having that debate within himself since he'd found her in Room 00. Finally Trigger shook his gray head, turned away and walked toward the open door. "I'll go to the county sheriff and see what I can find out," he agreed. "Do you want me to bring anything when I come back?"

He didn't want the Marshal to come back. "I have everything we need in the trunk." He followed the Marshal out to the rental car and groaned when he saw the fresh damage on it. "I'm definitely not getting my deposit back," he murmured as he got the box of food and clothes. Then he told the Marshal, "You've got my number. Call me as soon as you talk to the sheriff."

Trigger nodded and got back behind the wheel of the running car. When he drove off, he left the cottage and property in total darkness. Aaron stumbled his way to the open door and stepped into the blackness inside the home. As he did, a cold barrel pressed hard against his temple. Had the guards already tracked them down?

Maybe they should have followed Charlotte's instincts and gotten far away from Serenity House. He'd gotten her out, but he hadn't done a very damn good job of keeping her safe. He shifted the box to one arm, so he could nonchalantly reach for his gun.

"Don't move," a raspy voice warned him, "or I'll kill you."

Chapter Six

"You don't want to kill me," the man told her.

Timmer was right. She didn't want to kill him. But he was the only thing that stood, literally blocking the door, between her and freedom. And she suspected that she needed to leave before the other man returned.

What had he been saying about a case and a missing witness? And why had his mentioning those things had her heart beating heavy with dread and fear?

"I won't kill you," she promised, "as long as you do what I tell you. Hand over your gun and don't try to stop me from leaving."

"You can't leave," he said.

"Why did you go to the trouble of breaking me out of that place?" she asked. "Why take me out of one prison cell if you only intended to put me in another?" That was why she'd been determined to not get on that plane to only the devil knew where—the devil who claimed to be the father of her unborn child. She shuddered.

"This isn't a prison cell," he replied.

"Then let me leave."

"And go where?" he challenged her. "Do you have any idea where we are?"

"Too close to that horrible hospital." She shuddered again.

"Do you even know which state we're in?"

"We're in the U.S.?" The question slipped out, revealing too much of her ignorance. Hell, talking to him at all when she should have been running from him was showing her ignorance. She couldn't trust him—not when she couldn't remember who he was to her—besides that he was an old lover.

He nodded, his head moving against the barrel of the gun she held on him. She eased back a little, not wanting to hurt him. "We're in Michigan."

Michigan. She'd been in Michigan before. Hadn't she?

"And," he continued, "this place is a temporary shelter."

Despite her earlier threat, he moved. His eyes must have adjusted to the faint light as thick clouds moved away from a sliver of the moon. He set the box down on a table and rummaged inside it. If he'd been looking for a weapon, he would have pulled the gun from the waistband of his pants. Instead he pulled out a small box and a wad of paper, and he moved again—to the fireplace. The paper rustled then caught the flame from the match he struck. The paper ignited the logs that had been left in the hearth.

Warmth and light spilled from that wide brick hearth, tempting her to leave the bone-chilling cold of the open doorway and approach it. But then she'd be approaching him, too.

"We'll stay here," he said, "until we figure out our next move."

"Our next move should be getting out of this place," she said. They needed to leave before the older man returned or those guards from the hospital tracked them down.

"We have no vehicle," he pointed out.

She shouldn't have let the other man leave with the car, but she hadn't wanted to deal with him and his insistent questions, either. That was why she'd faked the faint. "I can walk."

"You're not strong enough," he said.

Pride lifted her chin. "I'm strong—"

"You just—" He stopped himself and laughed. "You didn't really faint. You staged that whole thing, so you could get the jump on me. I helped you escape Serenity House. Why won't you trust me?"

Serenity House? That was the name of the psychiatric hospital? How ironic when she'd felt anything but serene there.

"Because I don't know who you are," she reminded him.

"My name is Aaron Timmer."

She shrugged. "Your name means nothing to me." But that was a lie. *Aaron* felt right, like it fit him—like she had once fit him.

He sighed with obvious resignation. "You really don't remember anything."

"I need more than your name," she explained. "I need to know who you are. What kind of person can break in and out of a secure facility and steal an ID badge and fight off trained guards…?"

"A trained bodyguard," he replied.

"Bodyguard?" she asked, the title striking a chord within her. "For hire?"

"Yes, I'm a professional bodyguard. I used to have my own security business." He sighed again. "Well, with a partner, but that didn't work out. Now I protect only one person."

"Me?"

"No."

She smiled. "Good. Because if you were responsible for protecting me, you're not that great at your job."

He flinched as if she'd struck a nerve.

She nearly apologized, but then she didn't know the whole story. Didn't even know if what he was telling her was just a story and not the truth.

"If you're someone else's bodyguard, why are you here?" she asked. "Why did you come looking for *me?*"

AARON HAD ANSWERED her earlier questions because he wanted to jar her memory—wanted to say something that would have her remembering everything. So he'd been honest with her. But being honest now would gain nothing. She didn't know how he'd felt about her. Because she'd left the palace the morning after they'd made love, he hadn't even had time to figure out how he'd felt about her before she and the princess had disappeared.

"Why did you track me down?" she repeated her question. Then she drew in an audible breath and asked, "Or aren't I the woman you were looking for?"

"You're the woman I was looking for," Aaron assured her.

Her brow furrowed in skepticism. "I'm Princess Gabriella?"

"No," he said, correcting her. She was nothing like the princess, who he'd found to be rather timid despite having lived her life in the bright glare of the media spotlight. "You're Charlotte Green."

Her brow furrowed even more with confusion and skepticism. "You convinced the other man that I wasn't."

"I wasn't sure he can be trusted."

"I'm sure he can't," she said.

"You remember him?"

"I don't have to remember him to realize that he can't be trusted," she said. "I'm not sure I can trust you, either."

"I'm telling you the truth. You're Charlotte Green." He had no doubt. She may have forgotten who she was but she hadn't forgotten *what* she was. She wasn't just defending herself as she'd taught Princess Gabby; she was using her talent and experience to protect herself. She'd even used it to protect him back at Serenity House. "You're a bodyguard, too."

"I'm a bodyguard." She said it as if trying on the job title to see if it fit.

"Now," he said. "Before you went into private security, you were a U.S. Marshal."

"That's why that other man was talking about a case and a witness," she said. It was as if she was trying to fit together puzzle pieces to get a picture of her forgotten past.

He studied her face, looking for any flicker of recognition—to see if she remembered any of what he was telling her. "He thinks you know where she is."

"I don't know…" She lifted her free hand and rubbed her swollen temple as if her head was throbbing. "I don't remember…"

"That's okay," he assured her with a twinge of guilt for overwhelming her with information. It was obviously too much for her to process all at once. "He was talking about an old case. You may not know anything about that witness anymore."

"But the other guy—*Trigger*—" she uttered his nickname with such derision it was almost as if she did remember him "—said that the witness was a friend of mine."

"I haven't known you long," he admitted, "but it seems like you tend to become friends with the people you protect."

"Do you get close to the people you protect?" she asked.

He glanced back at the flames flickering in the hearth, and with a flash of pain he remembered another fire. "Sometimes too close and then it hurts too much when you lose them."

"Who's lost?"

He wouldn't talk about his old case with her. That wasn't her memory to recover, and it was one he wished he could forget. "Princess Gabriella."

"Is that who you were protecting?" she asked.

Aaron shook his head. "No, you're her bodyguard. Do you know what happened to her?"

She swayed as if her legs were trembling, as if she were about to pass out again. Or for real this time. Because she still tightly clutched the gun, he walked slowly and carefully toward her—trying to be non-threatening. But she didn't let him get close. Instead she moved around him to stand in front of the fireplace. She trembled yet, shivering.

Cold air blew through the open door, stirring sparks in the fire. So she stepped back from the hearth, as if afraid of getting burnt.

Aaron shut and locked the door, but because his kick had broken the jamb, he also moved a bureau in front of it to keep the wind from blowing it open again.

"Are you okay?" he asked, as he joined her by the

couch in front of the fireplace. "Is your memory coming back?"

She shook her head and grimaced. "No. It's almost like it's slipping farther away. If you're so sure I'm Charlotte and not the princess, then you're saying I had plastic surgery to look exactly like her? That's why you and that other man—that Marshal—didn't know for certain which one of us is which?"

Firelight flickered across her face, illuminating her perfect features—her breath-stealing beauty. "When you started protecting Princess Gabriella, you had plastic surgery to look like her. When I met you, you had already had it done—the two of you are pretty much identical." But only Charlotte had stolen his breath—not the princess.

"So identical that you couldn't tell us apart? What makes you so certain that you're right now?" she challenged him.

"I was wrong to doubt myself before," he said, self-disgust overwhelming him. "I should have known immediately that you were Charlotte."

"Why should you have known?" she asked.

He had to *tell* her. He just hoped she wouldn't laugh as she had at her old partner. Or worse yet deny that it had ever happened. "I should have known who you were right away because we were lovers."

LOVERS.

Those images—of his naked skin rippling over hard muscles—flashed through Charlotte's mind again. He wasn't lying to her. But maybe he didn't know the truth. "How can you be sure?" she asked.

He chuckled. "No one hit me on the head. I haven't lost my memory. We made love." He glanced down at her stomach, as if trying to gauge if the child she carried was his.

Was he the father? Another man claimed the baby was his. But she couldn't be any more certain that he was right than she could be sure of anything in this crazy situation.

"Why would Princess Gabriella's bodyguard have plastic surgery to look exactly like her?" she prodded him. This was one answer she knew but needed to draw him to the same conclusion she had.

"To protect her," he automatically replied, probably thinking she was stupid in addition to having amnesia.

"How?" she persisted. "By *fooling* someone into thinking that she was the princess even though she wasn't? By stepping in for the princess in the case of danger?"

He gave a slow nod, his blue eyes narrowing.

"Well, then," Jane said, bringing home her point, "when the bodyguard is pretending to be the princess, isn't the princess pretending to be the bodyguard?"

His jaw dropped open, as if he were appalled at the thought of being fooled into making love with the wrong woman. "No. I would have known. You're very different from the princess."

"You told the other guy that Charlotte taught the princess how to act like her."

"Just how to shoot and defend herself," he clarified, "but you're not Princess Gabby."

"How can you be so certain," she wondered, "when *I* don't know which woman I am?"

A muscle twitched in his jaw as if he was clenching it. "I wouldn't have gotten involved with a client."

"I thought you weren't the princess's bodyguard."

"I wasn't. I'm her father's bodyguard, so I wouldn't

have gotten involved with his daughter." His gaze dropped from hers as he made this claim.

She'd struggled to trust him before, but now she knew she shouldn't. "You're lying to me."

"Not lying—leaving something out."

Somehow she suspected she could relate—that she'd kept secrets of her own and had kept them so well that she couldn't even remember them now—when she so desperately needed to remember.

"What are you leaving out?"

"Something that happened before I met you." He uttered a ragged sigh. "Something that has nothing to do with you."

He sounded as if he believed that, but still she doubted him. He might not be aware of it, but she felt as though she had had something to do with it—something to do with whatever had his shoulders slumping even now with a heavy burden of guilt and regret. Guilt and regret overwhelmed her now. Her legs weakened and began to shake.

He reached for her, his hands on her arms steadying her. "Sit down," he advised, as he helped her settle onto the couch on which he'd laid her earlier. "You're probably starving. Let me get you something to eat."

"I don't need food," she said even as her stomach growled and the baby shifted inside her.

He headed back to the box and ripped open a plastic bag and then passed it to her. "It's just crackers. But there's soup in here, too. I can see if the stove works or heat it over the fire."

More out of reflex than hunger, she ate a couple of crackers. "This is fine," she assured him. "What I really need is my memory back. Since you didn't know for certain if I was Charlotte or the princess, you didn't know where *either* woman was."

"No," he said. "You've been missing for the past six months."

"I disappeared in Paris?"

"You remember?"

She shook her head. "You mentioned it in the car. It sounded ominous."

His jaw tensed again. "The hotel suite was trashed. There was evidence of gunshots. And blood. You must have been attacked."

She touched her swollen temple. "This isn't six months old."

"Do you have other scars or bruises?"

"Lots of them," she said. Either she'd been assaulted or tortured…maybe from someone trying to find out where the princess was. She had to be Charlotte. How would a princess, no matter how good her teacher, know how to shoot as she had? And the very thought of her being a princess was really utterly ridiculous…

He grimaced as if feeling the pain she must have felt when she'd gotten all those marks on her body. "You had some scars and bruises before you disappeared."

"I did?" She lifted her hand to her cheek, but the skin was smooth. It hadn't always been. She could almost remember running her fingertips over the ridge of a jagged scar.

He reached out and ran his fingertips along her cheekbone, as well. "You remember the scar…"

Her skin tingled from his fleeting touch. And she involuntarily leaned closer, wanting more—wanting to be closer to him. "I don't know if it's memory or instinct," she admitted. "Like with the gun, I didn't necessarily remember how to shoot—I just *knew*."

"That's how I know you're Charlotte. You can be sure of that, too," he said. "Princess Gabby has never even been in so much as a car accident. She would have no scars."

"We don't know that anymore," she said. "We don't know what happened to her." She could be dead, and that horrible thought overwhelmed Charlotte with grief. The princess must have been her friend. "How could I have failed to protect her?"

"You don't know that you failed her. You don't know that she's gone," he said, trying to offer her hope—which she feared might prove false. "Until the hotel in Paris called about the damaged suite, we thought that you two had run away."

She snorted derisively. "I must be at least thirty years old. I doubt we would have run away like teenagers." Then she remembered what Aaron had said when he'd first come into her room at the psychiatric hospital. "You thought I would be mad at you about some announcement the king had made…?"

He contorted his mouth as if biting the inside of his cheek—as if trying to grapple with what he'd done. Or what he'd allowed to be done. "The king is old-fashioned."

"He's a king—that's pretty archaic."

"To us Americans, yes," he agreed, "but in St. Pierre, he is the absolute authority. The ruler. He treats his daughter the same way he does his country. From the day she was born, she was betrothed to the prince of a neighboring island."

Anger flared inside her. "That is barbaric."

"I think she was resigned to marry Prince Demetrios," Aaron said. "But then the night of the ball…"

His pupils enlarged, darkening his pale blue eyes, as he remembered something.

The night they'd made love?

"What happened the night of the ball?" she asked.

"The king cancelled Gabriella's betrothal to Prince Demetrios."

"That's great—"

"And promised her to another," Aaron continued as if she hadn't spoken at all. "He changed her engagement to Prince Malamatos, whose country has more resources and wealth."

A curse spilled from Jane's lips—a curse she doubted a princess would know. "The king sounds like a selfish son of a bitch. Why would anyone work for him?"

"He's a powerful man who's used to getting what he wants."

"But his daughter disappeared before he could arrange her marriage," she said. "He must be furious."

"At first he was," Aaron admitted. "But then when the hotel notified us, he was devastated. He loves his daughter."

She snorted in derision of a man claiming to love someone he tried so hard to control. Jane's heart swelled with sympathy and concern for the princess. "But if Gabriella was alive, wouldn't you or her father have found her before now?"

"It took me six months to find you," he said with a heavy sigh of frustration.

"But you weren't looking for me," she said. "You were looking for the princess."

"The king and his other bodyguard—they're looking for the princess—I was always looking for you."

Her pulse stuttered and then raced. "Because we were lovers?"

"I know that blow you took gave you amnesia, but…"

"It bothers you to think that I forgot." She needed to tell him the truth—that one of the few memories she had was of him.

"And I haven't been able to get you—and that night—out of my mind." He reached out again, to touch her belly.

The baby shifted, kicking against his palm. If she believed the conversation between the guard and who-ever he'd called, this baby wasn't Aaron's. She belonged to another man. She needed to tell him—needed to be honest with him about the little she did remember. But before she could open her mouth, his lips pressed against hers.

And whatever thoughts she'd had fled her mind. She couldn't think at all. She could only feel. Desire over-whelmed her. Her skin tingled and her pulse raced.

He deepened the kiss, parting her lips and sliding his tongue inside her mouth. He kissed her with all the passion she felt for him.

She moaned, and he echoed it with a low groan. Then his palms cupped her face, cradling the cheek she'd touched looking for a scar. And he pulled back.

"I'm sorry," he apologized, and his broad shoulders slumped as if he'd added to that load of guilt and regret he already carried. Or, actually, she had added to it. "I shouldn't have done that…"

"Why did you?" she wondered aloud. With a bruised face and ugly scrubs stretched taut over her big belly, she was hardly desirable.

Those broad shoulders lifted but then dropped again in a slight shrug. "I wanted you to remember me—to remember what we once were to each other."

Confession time had come. "I remember," she admitted, "that we were lovers."

"You remember me?"

"I remember making love with you." And after that kiss she wanted to do it again—wanted to cling to the one good memory she had of her life before waking up in that horrible hospital.

Desire heated his blue eyes. "I haven't been able to forget—not one single detail of that night. But you have amnesia—"

"That's all I remember. You—just you..." She pulled him back to her and kissed him desperately. He was the one connection to her past—to who she was. She needed him close—as close as a human being could get to another.

He kissed her, too—with his lips and his tongue and with a passion that matched hers.

Putting aside her weapon, she slid her hands over him—as she had in that vivid memory. In the dream-like vision, he had worn a tuxedo. She'd undone his bow tie and all the studs on his pleated shirt. Now she had only to pull his scrub shirt over his head and push down his drawstring pants.

But he groaned and pulled back again. "We can't do this..."

"Why not?" she asked and then teased him. "Worried that I might get pregnant?" Or was he disgusted that she was? To find out if that was the case, she pulled off her shirt.

But the passion didn't leave his face. Instead his pale blue eyes softened with awe, and he reached out trembling hands, running his palms over her belly.

She needed to tell him that the child probably wasn't his. But before she could open her mouth, he was kissing her again. His hands moved from her stomach to her breasts. When his thumbs flicked over her nipples, she cried out with pleasure. Her desire for him was so intense that she lost all control—lost all sense of time and place as she had lost her past. He was that one link to who she was—her anchor in a storm of emotion and doubt. She needed him like she needed air.

She pushed him back onto the couch. Then she wriggled out of her pants and straddled him, taking him deep inside her. She cried out again, passion overwhelming her.

"Charlotte," he said with a deep groan. Muscles tensed in his shoulders and arms as he held her hips. He thrust gently, as if trying not to hurt her.

But she was beyond pain. Pleasure was all she felt in his arms, with him buried deep inside her. And finally he joined her in ecstasy, groaning gruffly as he filled her. She collapsed onto his chest, which heaved with pants for breath. But instead of relaxing like she had, his body tensed.

"Someone's here."

She tensed, too, as she heard gravel crunching beneath footsteps on the driveway. "It's probably that Marshal coming back."

"No. We have a signal he's supposed to give if it's him. Someone else is here."

"Maybe the owner of the cottage…" But she doubted it. They'd been found. And they might not even have time to get dressed and armed before the person, who rattled the door now, caught them.

Chapter Seven

Damn it. Damn him!

Aaron cursed himself for doing it again—for letting his emotions distract him. And his emotions for Charlotte were stronger than he'd ever had before. For anyone else. After helping her pull on her clothes, he pressed her down in front of the couch, even though the thin fabric and wooden frame would provide little protection from a barrage of bullets.

But he wouldn't give the intruder time to aim his gun. The minute the door opened he vaulted over the couch and tackled the dark figure, dragging him to the floor. He threw a punch, eliciting a grunt of pain. But the man swung back, striking Aaron in the jaw.

To block more blows, he locked his arms around the intruder's. Trying to break free of Aaron's hold, the guy bucked and rolled them across the floor toward the fire. The wood floor was hard beneath Aaron's bare back, scratching his skin. He'd only had time to pull on his pants before the stranger had broken the lock on the door. As they wrestled, Aaron's bare foot struck the hearth. Pain radiated up his leg, distracting him so that the man loosened his grip and swung his fist again.

In the light of the fire, Aaron recognized him. But

just as he said his name, "Whit," his former partner's dark eyes widened with shock before closing completely as he slumped forward—collapsing onto him.

Charlotte stood over the man, clenching the barrel of her gun in her hand. She'd struck Whit's head with the butt of the weapon, just as she had probably been struck when she'd lost her memory. "Who is he?"

"You don't recognize him?" Even if she had amnesia, Princess Gabriella probably would have. The young woman had seemed fascinated by her father's other bodyguard.

She studied the man's face before shaking her head. "No. Should I?"

"You've known him as long as you've known me," Aaron said, trying to prod her memory. But if making love hadn't brought it back…

"And how long is that?" she asked. Maybe the heat from the fire flushed her face or maybe she was embarrassed that she didn't remember how long she had known her lover.

"We met you just a couple of months before you and the princess disappeared," he replied. "His name is Whit Howell."

"And who is he?"

Aaron got up from the floor and stood over his old friend's unconscious body. "He is also one of the king's bodyguards."

"You work with him?"

He had sworn to himself that he never would again. But he had needed a real job—something more challenging than guarding white-collar secrets for corporations or vaults for banks. Choking on the self-disgust welling up in his throat, he just nodded.

"So we can trust him?" She dropped on her knees

beside Whit and felt for his pulse. Her breath shuddered out in a ragged sigh. "I didn't kill him."

"Good." Relief eased the pressure he hadn't even realized was squeezing his chest. No matter what he had become, Whit Howell had once been his friend. "But we really shouldn't trust him."

"Why not?"

Aaron shrugged. "It's kind of like your former partner—nothing I can prove—"

"If I could remember, I probably could prove that I can't trust that man," she said, glancing through the open door. "Your friend has a car out there. Grab his keys and let's get the hell out of here before the other guy comes back."

Aaron shook his head. "We can't leave yet." Maybe she was wrong about Trigger and the guy would come through with a subpoena for Serenity House's records. But he needed another answer right now and only one man could give him that. "I want to talk to Whit and find out how the hell he found me."

"If you two work together, didn't he know where you were going?"

"No. I made sure he didn't know," Aaron said. He had used a family emergency as his reason for leaving St. Pierre. Maybe Whit had checked out his story and discovered his lie. But how the hell had Whit tracked him down—not just to Michigan—but to this very cabin?

She glanced again out the open door. But darkness enveloped them in the impenetrable cocoon of night; morning was hours away yet. "We can take him with us and question him when he wakes up."

Aaron lifted Whit from the floor but just to drop his heavy body onto the couch. "I don't want him coming along with us. I don't want him to know where we're going." He already knew too much about Aaron's whereabouts.

She expelled an unsteady breath. "You *really* don't trust him."

"Not as far as I can throw him." He pointed toward the box. "There're some smelling salts in there. Can you find them?"

"Smelling salts?" She arched a golden-brown brow, as if offended. "You planned on me fainting?"

"You did," he retorted.

"Not for real."

The thought flitted unbidden into his head: What else had she faked? Amnesia? Desire? He shook off the idea; he didn't have time to deal with the consequences.

"There are some clothes in the box, too," he said. "You should probably change into something warmer." Spring nights were cold in Michigan, as a bitter gust blew through the open door.

She glanced down at the wrinkled scrubs and nodded. Then she lifted out the bundle of clothes. "Looks like some of these are yours."

"Yeah." Another cold gust blew through the open door, sending sparks shooting up the chimney. He caught the shirt and jeans she tossed at him.

"Here are the salts," she said, passing over a bottle. "I'll take these." She held on to a sweater and pants. "And change in another room."

"Why?" It wasn't like he hadn't already seen every inch of her. Again.

She pointed toward the man on the couch. "I didn't kill him, remember? He could come around even before you use those on him."

And Whit did. When a door to another room closed

behind her, the man shifted on the couch and groaned, struggling to regain consciousness. Aaron dragged on his jeans. He grabbed up the ID badges from Serenity House that he'd dropped on the floor in front of the couch when he'd torn off his clothes earlier. He might not need them again. But just in case he did…

As his head popped through the collar of the heavy knit shirt he pulled over his head, he came face-to-face with Whit. The guy's dark eyes were open and staring up at him. His brow furrowed with pain and confusion.

"Who hit me?" he asked, with another groan. "And what the hell did he hit me with?"

"Charlotte hit you with the butt of a gun," he replied matter-of-factly. After all, Whit wouldn't have followed him if he hadn't discovered he was chasing down a lead to her whereabouts.

"You found Charlotte?" Whit scrambled up from the couch and peered around the dimly lit room, as if looking for the female bodyguard. "And she's armed?" He slid his hand into his jacket, reaching for his own gun.

Aaron caught his arm. "What the hell's wrong with you?"

"What's wrong with you?" Whit asked. He pointed at the scratch on Aaron's forehead. "Did she do that? Did she shoot you?"

"It's nothing," he said, touching the mark on his head to remind himself. He'd forgotten all about the shard from the broken vase hitting him. "And she didn't do it. She isn't dangerous."

Whit uttered a bitter laugh. "There's no one more dangerous for you." He shook his head with disgust. "This is why you shouldn't have given me the slip back on St. Pierre. Family emergency—my ass."

"You were supposed to stay there and guard the

king," Aaron reminded him. As if he'd needed another reminder of why they were no longer business partners. "Who's protecting him? You didn't bring him with you?" He grimaced at the thought of the king in the line of fire. It was bad enough that Charlotte had been.

Whit shook his head. "He's still on St. Pierre, ensconced in the palace, with Zeke Rogers reinstated as head of his security in our absence."

"Zeke?" Aaron hadn't trusted the former mercenary and apparently neither had Charlotte since she'd recommended the king replace the man. "Is that wise?"

"With the guys we brought on as backup palace security, the king is safe," Whit assured him.

Were Aaron and Charlotte safe now that Whit knew where they were? Aaron asked the question that had been nagging at him since Charlotte had hit Whit over the head. "How did you find me?"

"Stanley Jessup."

Disappointment tugged at Aaron. Obviously the other man hadn't forgiven him. "He had promised me that he wouldn't tell you where I was."

It had been the most important of all the favors Aaron had requested of their former client.

"I forced it out of him," Whit defended the media mogul. The legendary businessman had never been forced into doing anything he hadn't wanted to—except for burying the ashes of his only child. "I told him you were playing white knight again, and that you were probably going to get yourself killed."

Even though Aaron had only gotten the scratch on his head and some bruises on his stomach, he couldn't deny that he had had some close calls. "None of that was Charlotte's fault. She's a victim in all this."

Whit shook his head. "No. Gabby is the real victim in all this. Did you find *her?*"

"No."

A muscle twitched in Whit's cheek, as if he'd tightly clenched his jaw. "Did Charlotte tell you what she did with her?"

Aaron hadn't been hit with anything other than that shard of glass or porcelain, but his head was beginning to ache. "What do you mean? What would Charlotte have done with Princess Gabriella? Do you think she's hidden her because of the king arranging another marriage for her?"

That muscle twitched in Whit's cheek again. "I thought so—at first," he admitted. "But even though Gabby might have been upset with her father, she loves him too much to make him worry this way. If she was all right, she would have contacted somebody by now."

"What makes you think Charlotte has anything to do with the princess not being able to contact anyone?" he said, wondering about Whit's suspicions. Was it Whit's cynicism talking or his own guilty conscience?

"She was the last one to see Gabby alive, so of course she had something to do with her disappearance. And I'm going to find out exactly what," Whit vowed, his dark eyes raging with anger and determination. "Where the hell is she?"

"She can't tell you anything," Aaron said, edging between Whit and the door which Charlotte had shut behind herself. Everyone wanted information from Charlotte. He wanted only Charlotte.

Whit was no longer the man who never gave in to—hell, even appeared to—have emotions. The anger bubbled over into pure rage. "She is damn well going to tell me what she did to Gabby!"

"She can't tell you anything!" Aaron shouted to get through to the stubborn man. He had never seen Whit so out of control. Maybe Charlotte had hit him too hard, like she had been hit too hard. "She doesn't remember."

Beneath the blond hair falling over his brow, furrows of confusion formed deep ridges. "Doesn't remember? What the hell are you talking about?"

"She has amnesia."

Whit stared incredulously at Aaron like he had just announced a spaceship landing on the island of St. Pierre. "What the hell—"

"She has a concussion," he explained. "She doesn't remember *anything*."

Whit snorted. "That's damn convenient. What doesn't she remember?"

"Anything. She doesn't remember anything." But him. "She doesn't even know who she is—if she's Charlotte or Gabby."

"And you fell for that?" Whit asked with a grimace of disgust.

"Why would she lie about something like that?" he asked because he had wondered, as well.

"Because the woman has lied to you about *everything*," Whit said. "Hell, she was lying to you before you even met her."

"What the hell are you talking about?" Aaron's stomach churned with a sick feeling of foreboding. "What has she lied to me about?"

That telltale muscle twitched in Whit's cheek. "Josie."

He fisted his hand, tempted to strike Whit again for even daring to mention the name of the woman who had died under their *protection*. "Josie? She didn't even know Josie Jessup."

"When Charlotte was with the U.S. Marshals, she staged Josie's death and relocated her," Whit said matter-of-factly, as if he was speaking the truth and not the wild fantasy that it had to be.

Aaron shook his head. "No. We were there—we both saw that house blow up."

"But we didn't see Josie in the house when it blew up," Whit pointed out. "Her body was never recovered."

"But her DNA…"

"Charlotte planted it and had a coroner identify the remains of a cadaver as Josie," Whit explained. "It was her last case before she discovered who her own father was. Then she realized she wouldn't ever have to work again if she played her cards right."

Aaron couldn't accept what Whit was saying. "Josie is dead."

"Nope," Whit corrected him. "She and Charlotte let you believe that."

"*You* let me believe that!" And of all the people who had known about Josie going into the witness relocation program, his best friend should have been the one to tell him the truth. *Then.* Not now…

Now it was too late—to undo the damage that had been done to their friendship—too late to restore the trust that Aaron had lost.

"When you saw how much he'd been suffering, you would have told Stanley Jessup," Whit said. "And no one could know where she was."

"Do you know?"

"Charlotte is the only one authorized to know her whereabouts," Whit replied. "Not even Charlotte's partner with the U.S. Marshals knows."

So Josie had to be the witness that Trigger had wanted to question Charlotte about—the one he claimed had gone missing. But how could he know that if he'd never known where she was?

"But I don't care about Josie," Whit said.

The admission surprised Aaron because he'd thought the other man had been as attracted to the American princess as he had been. Well, he'd thought that until Whit had talked him into leaving her momentarily un-protected. Now Aaron knew why he had—if he believed what the other man was telling him. Now. More than three years after the fact.

"I care about Gabby," Whit admitted. "I want to know what Charlotte did to her. Let me talk to her! Now!"

Aaron was afraid that talking wasn't all Whit in-tended to do to Charlotte. And Aaron hadn't found her only to lose her again.

But then had he ever really had her? Betrayal struck him like a fist in the gut. Did he have any idea who she actually was?

THIS MAN, THIS stranger who'd broken into the cottage—he knew Charlotte. He knew her better even than the man with whom she'd made love because Whit Howell knew all her secrets. All the secrets she hadn't really wanted to remember.

Aaron had been in love with another woman—so in love with her that he'd turned on his best friend. He'd given up his business. His life. He had been so in love with Josie Jessup that he would have never been able to fall for another woman.

No matter what feelings Charlotte might have had for him, they would never be returned. And now she heard the suspicion in his voice as he questioned his emotional friend.

"Why do you think Charlotte would hurt the princess? They were so close. She had surgery to look like her, to protect her!"

Charlotte closed her eyes, and the image was there—of her face. But it wasn't her face at all. The golden brown eyes were wide and full of innocence and naïveté. And the skin was so smooth, completely free of lines of old scars or stress. Princess Gabriella St. Pierre had spent her life so sheltered that she'd been completely unaware of what the world was really like.

It would have been so easy to take advantage of that youth and innocence. So easy to dupe her...

"Charlotte Green had surgery, so she could take over Princess Gabriella's life and her inheritance."

Aaron's derisive snort permeated the door behind which Charlotte stood. "That might have worked if everyone wasn't aware that she'd had that surgery. Everyone in the king's inner circle—his business associates, lawyers and financial advisors—knows Princess Gabriella has a doppelganger."

"Charlotte isn't just a doppelganger."

"No," Aaron agreed. "She's her bodyguard and her friend."

"She's her *sister*."

"No."

Charlotte silently echoed that denial. Sisters grew up together or were at least aware of each other's existence. Charlotte hadn't been until her mom had finally conned the wrong person and wound up dead, leaving behind documents that Charlotte had never seen before, documents that had proved that her mother's outrageous lies had actually been the truth.

"Why do you think they looked so much alike?" Whit asked.

"The surgery—"

"Hadn't changed her height or build or coloring," Whit pointed out. "Even before the surgery they'd looked eerily similar."

"How do *you* know?" Aaron asked and then bitterly answered his own question, "Oh, that's right, you met her before…when you helped her stage Josie's *death*."

Jealousy kicked Charlotte in the stomach just as the baby did. Why had she given in to her attraction to him even though she had known that he had already given his heart to another? She patted her belly soothingly.

Apologetically…

"She's good at staging murder scenes," Whit said.

"Like Paris?"

"Maybe that wasn't staged," Whit said. "Maybe that was a real murder scene. Maybe she killed Gabby."

"I don't think—"

"No, man, you don't!" Whit accused him. "You *feel*. And you let those feelings cloud your judgment. That's why you couldn't know about Josie."

"Why couldn't I know about *Charlotte?*" he asked, his voice gruff with anger. "Why didn't you tell me that she's the king's daughter, too?"

"Because King St. Pierre didn't want anyone to know."

Charlotte flinched, feeling rejected all over again. Her father hadn't wanted his dirty little secret to come out. But he'd been happy to use her to protect the daughter he had wanted. The one he had loved.

"And that's why she did this," Whit explained. "With his legitimate heir dead, he'll be forced to acknowledge his illegitimate one—if he wants to continue his reign in St. Pierre."

"Charlotte wouldn't do something like that," Aaron protested, but his argument had weakened, his voice lower now with doubt.

She had to nearly press her ear against the wood to hear him.

"You don't know Charlotte Green at all," Whit said, almost gently. "You have no idea what she's capable of…"

But Charlotte finally did—as all of her memories came rushing back over her. They struck her like blows. And as the pain overwhelmed her, she wanted to strike back.

Fists clenched at his sides, Aaron struggled for control. He wouldn't hit Whit—despite his gut-wrenching need to pummel the other man until he took back every last word he'd uttered.

"You have no proof to back up all these wild accusations." His head reeled from them, making him wonder if he had been hit harder than a graze. "Why should I believe you?"

"Because I always had your back," Whit said. "Because we were closer than friends—we were like brothers."

"Until Josie…" Losing her had cost them their friendship. But then they hadn't really lost her.

"There was nothing between me and her, you know," Whit said.

Aaron had thought there'd been, and he'd resented Whit for acting on the attraction Aaron had struggled to ignore. Because he'd wanted to be professional, had wanted to keep her safe. And all these years he'd thought he'd failed. "It doesn't matter now."

Because he realized those feelings for Josie hadn't been real. He'd liked her, had admired her beauty and brains, but he hadn't loved her. He'd only loved one woman, but now that might have been a lie, too.

If he were to believe Whit…

"What you're saying is wrong," Aaron pointed out. "None of it makes sense."

"Greed always makes sense," Whit insisted, his words an unwitting reminder of how much money had mattered to him. His background was completely opposite Aaron's; Whit had grown up poor with a single dad who'd struggled to support them. Whit had been denied all the things he'd wanted. Had he gotten sick of going without all the things that money could buy—all the things he'd always considered so important?

"But if she'd intended to pull the switch, why had she talked the king into hiring us?" Aaron wondered.

"Maybe the king's head of security had been on to her," Whit suggested. "Maybe she thought we would be easier to dupe than the guard who'd known Gabriella her whole life."

At Serenity House, Aaron had had his doubts about her identity. And she and the princess had disappeared just a couple of months after he and Whit had been hired. "I can't believe this…"

"Let's ask her," Whit suggested. "Get her out here to explain herself."

She wouldn't be able to explain what she couldn't remember. But was Whit right? Had her claim of amnesia just been a trick? Was it all a trick? His legs didn't feel quite steady as he walked across the room to that closed door. "Charlotte?"

She didn't reply. She had probably heard every word of their conversation—why hadn't she come out earlier to explain herself? He reached for the knob, but it wouldn't turn. She'd locked him out. Like he had the front door, he kicked the door until it broke free of the jamb.

Cold air, flowing through an open window, hit him in the face like a shotgun blast.

"She's gone?" Whit asked, leaning against the broken jamb behind Aaron.

He shut his eyes as dread pummeled him. "Tell me you didn't leave the keys in the car."

Whit cursed profusely. They both turned toward the front door—just in time to see the flash of a gun as it fired directly at them.

He'd been such a fool—such a damn fool to fall for her lies. To fall for her. And now he was about to become a dead fool…

Chapter Eight

As he had just minutes ago, Aaron knocked Whit to the ground again. Bullets flew over their heads and filled the room. Stuffing burst from the holes in the couch and wood splintered—in the furniture and the walls behind them. And the sound was deafening, rattling the windows and shaking the pictures off the walls.

It wasn't a handgun firing at them—more likely a machine gun or some other automatic rifle. Even if they could get off a shot, they were outgunned.

"We have to get the hell out of here!" Aaron said. When he'd first found the cabin, he had scoped it out and knew all the exits. He dragged Whit across the floor with him, toward the back door. It was the one he'd left unlocked earlier. But instead of reaching up to turn the knob, he just kicked it open as he had the others.

"She took my car, man," Whit reminded him, as they rolled across the back porch and tumbled down the steps.

Aaron kept low to the ground as they edged around the corner of the cottage. How long before the shooter stormed inside and discovered them gone? Minutes? Seconds? "And your gun?"

"I have my gun on me." It glinted in that sliver of

moon. He had it drawn, clutching it tightly in his hand. "She had her own. She hit me with it," Whit reminded him.

"That's not her gun shooting at us." Where was Charlotte? They hadn't heard the car start; she may not have driven off before the gunman arrived. She could have been somewhere out there—in the line of fire? Or kidnapped again. "We have to make sure she's okay."

"She's okay," a female voice whispered. "This way…"

Aaron turned to follow the shadow moving toward the trees, but Whit caught his arm.

"Don't trust her," he warned, lifting his gun so that the barrel pointed toward her.

Aaron knocked the gun down. "She's not the one shooting at us."

That person had moved to the back of the building. More shots rang out, hitting the ground near them.

They ran toward the woods. Aaron easily caught up to Charlotte. She wasn't as strong as she wanted to be, and her gait was unsteady. He caught her around the waist, almost carrying her through the small thicket of brush.

"I parked the car over here," she said.

It idled in the dark, its lights shut off. The engine was quiet. No wonder Aaron hadn't heard it drive up or drive away.

"You stole my car," Whit accused as he opened the driver's door and slid in behind the wheel.

As she scooted across the backseat in front of Aaron, she nodded. "I took it. But when I saw the other car driving toward the cottage, I came back." She turned to face Aaron, her gaze steady, as if she was trying to tell him something else. "I came back…"

Before she could explain herself, the back window exploded behind her. Aaron pushed her head down below the seat.

Whit slammed the car into Drive and pressed hard on the accelerator. Gravel sprayed from under the wheels as the car fishtailed, nearly careening into the trees surrounding it.

Aaron checked Charlotte. Shards of glass caught in her hair, cutting his fingers as he brushed them out. "Are you all right?"

"Do you care?" she asked, and she drew back, settling into the corner and probably for more than protection. Obviously she'd heard quite a bit of his discussion with Whit before she'd climbed out the window and stolen the only means of escape.

But she came back, he reminded himself. And somehow he suspected she meant more than physically.

"What the hell is this road?" Whit grumbled as the car bounced over deep ruts.

As well as the cabin, Aaron had scoped out the area surrounding it before he and Trigger had gained access to Serenity House. "It's the public access road to a lake."

"A lake?" Whit repeated. "So if I keep going we're going to hit water?"

And the road was unlit, the surrounding woods dark, blocking out that faint sliver of moon. They might not even see the lake before it was too late and the car was going under.

"Turn around," Charlotte advised.

But bright lights came up fast behind them—blinding in the rearview mirror.

"Get down," Aaron said, as he pulled Charlotte onto the floorboards behind the front seats. He covered her with his body, protecting her from flying glass and gunfire.

But if they were forced off the road into the lake, he wasn't sure he would be able to save her then. He wasn't sure he would be able to save himself in dark, cold water.

But hell, he already felt as though he was drowning—going under from all the information Whit had given him—from all the secrets his old partner had revealed. Aaron was already drowning in emotion, so water couldn't hurt him much more.

SHE HAD ALREADY hurt him enough—with all the secrets she'd kept from him. She couldn't accept this, too—his using his own body to protect hers. But maybe he wasn't really protecting her—maybe he was protecting the child he thought was his.

And there was one more secret she'd kept from him. "I'm sorry," she murmured, turning her face into his neck as he crouched over her.

His heart thumped fast and hard in his chest; she felt each beat of it against her back—beating in rhythm with hers. They would have been perfect for each other—if he hadn't already loved another woman.

But Charlotte was used to that—used to being rejected for someone sweeter and prettier—someone more uncomplicated and open. Her own father had rejected her in favor of her sister, choosing Gabriella as his heir even though Charlotte was his firstborn.

She covered the rounded swell of her belly. She didn't care who the father of her child was; she wouldn't reject her. Charlotte would never deem a baby unworthy of her love.

But Aaron probably would—were he to learn the

truth. She needed to tell him—needed to tell him *everything*. Because she remembered...

But she couldn't talk into his neck as they huddled in the backseat. She had to wait until they got to safety. If that was even possible...

"You have to do something," Aaron ordered his former friend. "If we go in that water, we'll be sitting ducks. He'll just wait until we surface to shoot us dead."

"You don't think I know that?" Whit snapped, his voice gruff with frustration.

"We're braced back here," Aaron said. "Put on your seat belt and then slam on the damn brakes. Hard."

"He'll rear-end us," Whit said.

"Yeah," Aaron agreed. "And maybe he'll knock himself right through the windshield or at least the hell out."

Charlotte nodded her approval of the plan. They were safer on land than in the water—had more options for escape.

But then the car screeched to a stop, and the other car struck them with a sickening crunch of metal. Despite Aaron holding her tight, she shifted against the seats and her shoulder jammed into the console.

"Are you okay?" Aaron asked.

She managed only a nod.

Then Whit shoved the car into Reverse and stomped on the accelerator. Bumper ground against bumper, as the pursued became the pursuers.

Aaron rose up, and his gun glinted in the headlamps of the other car. But instead of becoming a target again, he took aim and fired. Again and again.

If he didn't hit his target, he would become one. And the driver of the other car had a clear shot at him. Charlotte reached up, trying to pull him down—trying to protect him as he had protected her.

The metal crunched against metal again. Rubber burned, enveloping the cars and woods in a thick, acrid smoke. Charlotte blinked furiously against the sting, fighting off the threat of tears so that she could see—so that she could make sure Aaron was all right.

But there was another crash that flung Aaron's body into the back of the front seat. He grunted and struggled for the grip on his gun. But it flew into the front, leaving him unarmed and vulnerable.

Charlotte pulled her weapon from the back of her jeans, but by the time she surged up—it was too late. There was nothing she could do...

"Is HE REALLY gone?" Whit asked, as he stood over Aaron's body. Instead of gazing down at his friend, he stared off down the road in the direction the other vehicle had disappeared.

Aaron scrambled to his feet. He'd had to crawl out of the crumpled rear door of the backseat he'd shared with Charlotte. The trunk was totally crushed, and the quarter panels had buckled. "For now."

"Do you think you hit him?" Whit asked.

Aaron shook his head. "If I did, it wasn't fatal or even painful enough to stop him."

"It got him to leave though," Whit remarked.

"He'll be back." Every time the mysterious gunman had fired at Aaron, the man had come back for another round.

Whit moved back toward the open driver's door. "Then we should get the hell out of here."

Aaron wanted to make sure Charlotte was okay first. He reached back and helped her out of the twisted metal. "Are you all right?"

He found himself reaching out automatically to her

belly, placing his hands on her to check her baby as if he had the right. As if the baby was his…

Was it?

They'd used protection that night—and they had only been together just that one night. Until tonight…

And letting her distract him had nearly taken all their lives. The baby moved beneath his palms, kicking against her belly.

"I'm fine," she said. "But Whit's right. We need to get out of here before he comes back."

"We're going to need time to find a safe place," Aaron said. He couldn't risk her and her unborn child getting into the line of fire again.

"Got it," Whit said.

Doubt knotted Aaron's stomach muscles. Over three years ago he had lost his trust of this man. And learning that Whit had lied to him hadn't exactly worked to regain that trust. "You just got here." Hadn't he? "How do you already know of a safe place to stay?"

"Stanley Jessup."

"He found you a place?" All he'd given Aaron was the name of the hospital where Princess Gabby might have been committed. Okay, he'd given him a hell of a lot.

"His place."

"Stanley Jessup has a place here?"

Whit nodded. "He rented something. He's here. Guess he wanted to see for himself if this story was as big as that freelance reporter claimed it would be."

It was a hell of a lot bigger, and Aaron didn't even know the half of it. The woman who did was, of course, keeping quiet. Keeping her secrets…

So many damn secrets…

And he had so many questions. He kept them to himself during the bumpy and rigorous ride in the damaged car to the cottage Stanley Jessup had rented. It was nothing like the cabin Aaron had found in the woods near Serenity House.

The contemporary tower of metal and glass sat on a dune overlooking Lake Michigan. Waves rushed to the dark shore below, breaking apart on the rocks. While Whit had gone inside the house, Charlotte stood on the overlook deck, her arms propped on the railing.

Aaron joined her on that deck that overlooked the beach far below. But he kept a careful distance from her. "Don't you have anything to say?" he wondered out loud.

Like sorry?

Charlotte shrugged. "I've been waiting for the inquisition. It sounded like your friend has a lot of questions for me."

"More like a lot of accusations." He glanced toward the house, where a shadow moved behind one of the walls of glass. "Is that why you ran?"

Or was it because she'd gotten caught in a web of her own lies?

"Does it matter why I left?" she asked. "I came back…" Her tone was just as distant as it had been before.

"It matters to me," he said. Why she'd left and why she'd returned…

Even knowing how much she'd lied to him, she mattered to him. Self-disgust over what a lovesick fool he was turned his stomach.

"I was overwhelmed," she said. "It all came back. All my memories."

"Had they ever really been gone?"

She sucked in a breath, as if offended that he wouldn't

trust her. Given what he'd learned, how the hell could he trust her? No matter what she told him now…

"I didn't remember anything," she insisted. "But you…"

His heart—his stupid, traitorous heart—clenched in his chest. "I can't believe you," he said. "I can't believe anything you tell me now."

"But you can believe *him?*" she asked. "Hasn't he lied to you, too?"

He found himself defending his old friend. "Because you made him."

"Does anyone make Whit Howell do something he doesn't want to do?" she asked with a bitter chuckle.

No. But she didn't need the confirmation. She already knew.

"So you do remember everything now?" he asked.

"No," she replied with a shaky sigh of frustration. "There are still holes in my memory."

"Paris?" They needed to know what had happened there, if they were ever to learn Princess Gabriella's fate.

"I remember someone bursting into the suite, guns blazing. I remember fighting for my life. And then I woke up in that damn hospital." She touched her stomach. "Pregnant…"

That was a hell of a hole. How many months had she lost?

He drew in a breath, bracing himself for the answer before he even asked the question. "Do you remember who the father of your baby is?"

Her reply was a flat, unemotional "No." As if it didn't matter to her.

And it mattered like hell to Aaron. "So it might not be mine?"

She shook her head. "She's probably not."

He had known about the child for less than twenty-four hours but losing her—losing the possibility that she was his—hurt like hell. The loss twisted something inside Aaron, tied his emotions up in a tight knot.

"When Mr. Centerenian, that guard, called whoever the hell his boss is, he referred to the person as the father," she explained.

That breath he'd drawn in to brace himself stuck in his lungs, hurting his chest. "So you knew that I wasn't the father before I broke you out of Serenity House? Before we…" He couldn't call it making love—not now that he had confirmation that only his feelings had been involved.

"I was confused and scared. I had no idea what was going on. I didn't even know who I was. You were the only one I recognized, making love with you was the only thing I remembered."

She turned toward him and closed the distance between them. Wrapping her arms around him, she clung to him as if she cared—as if his feelings might not have been all one-sided. "I needed you…"

Aaron released the breath he'd held, but the pressure in his chest didn't ease. And the rest of his body tensed with attraction to her. No matter how many secrets she'd kept from him, no matter how many lies she'd told him—he still wanted her.

But he resisted the urge to wrap his arms around her and hold her close. Because he couldn't think with desire overwhelming him. He couldn't be objective when his emotions got involved; Whit had been right about that. *Damn him!*

So Aaron caught her shoulders in his hands and eased her away from him. "But now you have your memory back," he reminded her. "You don't really need me anymore."

He suspected Charlotte Green had never needed anyone. She was tough and independent. And those very traits that had drawn him to her were what would keep them apart.

"I still don't know who committed me to that horrible hospital."

That same person was the father of her child. "You have no idea who it could be?"

She had been in the princess's world longer than he had. She would know all the king's enemies. Not that he couldn't think of a few after the king's announcement at the ball the night before the princess and her bodyguard had left for Paris. But had the person who'd committed Charlotte to Serenity House realized she was Charlotte or had he mistaken her for Princess Gabriella?

She shook her head. "All I know for certain is that it wasn't me. I don't have some master plan to take my sister's place as princess of St. Pierre. I don't want that kind of life."

"You don't want a life of wealth and privilege?" he asked skeptically. "You just wanted her face?"

She skimmed her fingertips across her cheek that used to be marred with that horrific scar.

Aaron had only seen that one photograph of her face before the surgery, but the scar had haunted him, reminding him of the pain she must have endured when the injury had been inflicted. That snapshot had been of her and her aunt, their arms around each other—both looking, as Whit had said, eerily similar to Princess Gabriella, even before the surgery.

She tapped her cheek. "I did this to protect her—to keep her safe. I wouldn't have done anything to hurt

Gabby. Not like her father continuously hurt and betrayed her."

"*Her* father? But the king is your father, too."

She shook her head. "He's my employer. Not my father. And if not for Gabby, he wouldn't even be that. I wanted to protect her."

Maybe Whit was right again. Maybe Charlotte had hidden Gabby from the king—to thwart his plans to marry off the young princess. He studied her face, looking for any sign that she might be lying when he asked, "Where is she?"

She shook her head. "I don't know..."

Aaron shouldn't believe her—given how easily and often she'd lied and kept information from him in their brief past. But he wanted to believe her. He needed proof to do that. "I'll go back to Serenity House."

He had almost gotten into the administrator's records once. With more time, he could break into the system. Or maybe there was another way he could find out. He pulled his cell from his pocket and checked the call log. He hadn't missed any, though—not even during the shoot-out. "Trigger was going to try to get a warrant for their records. I'll see what he found out—"

Charlotte knocked the phone from his hand. The cell flew over the railing and dropped far to the beach below, breaking apart on the rocks.

Staring down at the pieces of metal and plastic glinting in the faint light of that crescent moon, he murmured, "What the hell—"

"Don't you get it?" she asked with impatience. "He can't be trusted."

"You remember him?"

"I remember that Trigger is actually short for Trigger *Happy*. He's a loose cannon. And there's another reason I didn't tell him where Josie is," she said. "He can be bought and the people looking for her have deep pockets."

He gasped. "She's still in danger?"

She turned away, looking out at the waves rushing toward the shore. "Too many people now know she's still alive."

He glanced toward the house but no lights had come on inside. Whit must not have woken Stanley Jessup yet. "So we can tell her dad the truth?"

"No," she said. "You shouldn't have been told, either. Every person that learns the truth puts her in more danger."

Aaron nodded.

He didn't like that he'd been lied to—that people thought he'd failed to protect his client. But if lying to him had kept her safe, he would make peace with the fact.

"Do you think that could have been Trigger shooting at us tonight?" he asked. It would explain why he hadn't called; why he hadn't come back...

She nodded, and her tangle of golden hair fell across her face. "If Mr. Centerenian hadn't found us, it could have been Trigger. He's one of the few who knew where we were."

"The only one who wasn't there when the shooting started," Aaron pointed out.

"But how did Whit know where we were?" she asked.

"Stanley Jessup told him," he reminded her.

"But he knew *exactly* where we were," she pointed out. "He knew we'd already broken out of Serenity House and broken into that very cabin to hide out. How did he know that?"

Aaron had wondered that himself and had fully intended to find out how—but then the shooting had started. "You think that Whit could be working with Trigger?"

"Or someone else he's had following you," she suggested, "maybe from the minute you left St. Pierre."

"But they shot at him, too."

"But he didn't get hit, did he?"

"You're saying I shouldn't trust the man I've known for so long." When sometimes he felt like he'd only known her ten minutes.

"Do you trust him?"

"Damn it..." His curse was his admission. He couldn't trust Whit. When she'd staged Josie's death, Charlotte hadn't known Aaron. But Whit had—he'd known how much it'd hurt him—how much it had hurt him to think he'd failed her. But he'd let him suffer anyways.

Whit was not really his friend.

"I should contact the authorities myself then," he said since he couldn't trust that the U.S. Marshal had.

"Serenity House might be the biggest employer around here. Someone at the sheriff's office could tip them off," she pointed out. "Then they'd have time to destroy the records."

She was smart, since Dr. Platt had insinuated as much when he'd been listening to her conversation with the private guard. He needed to accept that he could trust no one. "I'll go to Serenity House alone."

"No," she said. "I'm going with you."

"We barely got you out of that place," he reminded her. "We can't risk taking you back there."

"I know who I am now," she said. "I know how to take care of myself."

Even when she hadn't known who she was, she'd still known how to defend herself. And him.

"What about your baby?" he asked. Her baby. Not his. Why did it hurt so much to lose what he'd never really had? What he hadn't even realized he'd wanted? "Don't you want to take care of him?"

"Her," she corrected him—almost automatically. Every time she'd talked about the baby, she'd referred to her as a girl.

"You had an ultrasound," he realized. "You know what you're having?"

"If I had an ultrasound, I don't remember it," she said. "But I know…" She was already connected to her child.

"Then you know you have to stay here—where she will be safe." He didn't wait for her agreement. He didn't care what she said. She damn well wasn't going back to Serenity House with him.

Hoping that Whit had left the keys in his car again, Aaron headed toward the driveway. That sliver of moon led him toward the banged-up vehicle. It had a sticker on the crumpled rear bumper that identified it as being from the same rental company as Aaron's car. Whit wasn't going to get back his security deposit, either. With the rear quarter panels nearly pushed into the tires, it was a wonder that the thing was drivable at all.

But it had to make another trip. Aaron needed to discover the truth about how Charlotte had wound up in Serenity House. And he figured he was only going to trust it was true if he learned it for himself instead of trusting what someone—anyone—told him.

Charlotte had raised more doubt in his mind. About her. But mostly about Whit.

Could he trust what his former business partner had

claimed? And how had the man found him at the abandoned cabin tucked away in the woods?

Sure, he'd been with him when the shots had been fired. But that didn't mean he didn't have an accomplice—either the Marshal or some mercenary he'd hired. Had he wanted to kill Aaron and take Charlotte for ransom since he was one of the few who knew she was really royalty?

Had Whit known where to find them because he was the one who'd put her in Serenity House?

Aaron opened the door and the dome light glinted off the keys hanging from the ignition. After what had happened at the cabin, Whit really should have been more careful. Aaron slid behind the wheel and reached for the keys. But he didn't turn them. Because the barrel of a gun pressed against his temple.

He really should have been more careful.

Chapter Nine

In the rearview mirror, Aaron met Whit's gaze. "This is the second damn time that someone I thought I could trust pressed a gun to my head and threatened to kill me."

"I haven't threatened you."

Aaron pointed toward his head. "Guess it's kind of implied by the gun to my temple."

Whit pulled it away. "I thought you were her. I figured she'd give you the slip on the beach and try to steal the car again."

"Sure, she stole it. But she came back," Aaron reminded him.

"Probably to make sure we didn't get away from the guys she hired to kill us."

Aaron snorted. "She speaks highly of you, too."

"So she's talking now?" Whit scoffed. "Passing all the blame off on me?"

Aaron turned around to face his old partner. "She doesn't know who's to blame."

Whit snorted now. "Yeah, right."

"You didn't see her in Serenity House," Aaron said, flinching as he remembered how scared and confused she'd been. That was why he'd momentarily mistaken her for Princess Gabriella. "She was tied down to a bed. She had been beaten up and bruised. She didn't do that to herself."

"So who did it?"

Possibly Whit. He knew, as few people did, that Charlotte Green was a royal heir. "I'm going back to Serenity House to find out."

"You're just going to walk inside and politely ask them for the princess's records?" Whit scoffed. "At least I'm assuming they thought she was the princess since that's the tip the freelance reporter passed on to Stanley Jessup."

"How did the reporter get that tip?" Aaron hadn't bothered asking Jessup who his source was because the media mogul was a die-hard newsman and fanatic defendant of the First Amendment. He would never reveal a source.

"Someone on staff at Serenity House tipped off the young reporter," Whit explained. "Do you want me to wake up Stanley and get the reporter's contact information? He's some young kid fresh out of community college, but he's got great investigative skills. He's been following you around since you got here."

The kid was very good because Aaron usually figured out when he was being tailed. But maybe three years of being bored out of his mind in corporate security had dulled his instincts. "So that's how you knew where I was tonight?"

Whit nodded. "What? Did you think I planted a GPS chip in you like a dog?"

Aaron chuckled.

"I thought about it," Whit teased, reminding Aaron of the friend he had once trusted with his life. "But I thought you'd notice. And you probably wouldn't believe that you were abducted by aliens, and they implanted it."

Aaron snorted with derision. "I'm not that big a fool."

"You are if you think you're going to just waltz right back in there." Whit crawled over the console and dropped into the passenger seat. "I checked that place out. It's got higher security than most federal penitentiaries."

"That's why whoever kidnapped Charlotte put her in that place."

Whit stared at him with respect. "So how'd you get her out?"

Aaron pulled one of the ID badges from his pocket, grateful now that he'd grabbed them from the cabin. He suspected they hadn't been deactivated—just that during their escape someone had sounded an alarm that sealed all the doors and gates.

"I used this to get out, and I'll use it to get back in. It's like a key that'll let me through all the locked doors and gates." He dug deeper into his pocket. "I should have a couple more of these." He'd taken three.

"We only need one more," Whit said, holding out his hand—palm up, "for me."

Aaron's pocket was empty. "I must have lost them back at the cabin…"

"When we were getting shot at," Whit finished for him. "It's okay. Instead of splitting up and having me play the diversion tactic, we'll have to stick together at the hospital."

He was tempted. But he'd be a fool to trust anyone again. "Like I told Charlotte, it'll be better if I just go in alone."

"And she agreed to that?" Whit asked skeptically.

Aaron nodded. "She knows it's not safe for her to go back there."

"It isn't safe for you, either," Whit pointed out. "I should be the one to go back in alone. Let me do this…"

Aaron shook his head. "No."

Whit uttered a ragged sigh of resignation. "You still don't trust me."

"Right now I don't know who to trust," he replied, "not after years of being lied to."

The sigh became a groan. "God, man, I would have told you the truth if I could have. But you wouldn't have been able to watch Stanley Jessup suffer like he had and not tell him that his daughter wasn't dead. And the people after her needed to see him suffer to believe she was really gone. Don't you get that?"

Anger and resentment overwhelmed Aaron. "I get that you didn't trust me to do my job—to protect our client, and you let me suffer these past three years thinking that I'd failed."

"It wasn't like that…"

"It was exactly like that," Aaron retorted. "You didn't trust me. So how can you expect me to trust you?"

"Then don't let me go in alone," Whit negotiated. "But let me go in *with* you. We have always worked well together—in Afghanistan and running our own security business. Hell, look what we did tonight. You pulled me out of the line of fire."

"And you drove us here, to safety," Aaron had to admit.

Whit uttered a wistful sigh of nostalgia. "It was like old times…"

Aaron chuckled. "Yeah, getting shot at—running for our lives. It sure was like old times."

Whit chuckled. "I didn't say they were all good times."

"Okay, you can come along," Aaron allowed.

"You've finally decided you can trust me again?"

Aaron turned the keys in the ignition and pointed at the lightening sky. "I'm sick of arguing about it. We're wasting time. Our best chance of getting inside and finding the records is going to be now—before the more heavily staffed first shift starts."

The rental car's ignition whined but didn't turn over. However, another engine fired up, breaking the quiet of the late night. Lights momentarily blinded Aaron until the car passed them. And as it passed, Aaron recognized the profile of the woman driving the sports car.

"Charlotte..." She must have taken a car from the garage of Stanley Jessup's rental home. "I thought she agreed to stay here. Out of danger..." Aaron turned the keys again, but the engine refused to start. "Now she's going off with no backup..."

"Damn her," Whit said, pounding his fist against the dash. "She's getting away."

"She's not getting away," Aaron said. "She's going back to Serenity House. She's risking getting caught all over again."

Whit pounded the dash again—this time right in front of Aaron. "She told you she was staying here, too. Why would you believe anything *she* tells you?"

But, Aaron realized, she'd never actually said the words—had never agreed not to go back to Serenity House. Whit's pounding the dash must have knocked something loose because the car finally started.

"We have to beat her back there." Or she would walk alone into danger—just as she had so many times before.

Whit shook his head. "How many times do I have to tell you that you can't trust Charlotte Green?"

"I know I can't trust her," Aaron admitted. But he didn't want to lose her, either. And if she walked back into Serenity House alone, he worried that he would.

SHE HAD BEATEN them to Serenity House. The car she'd borrowed from the garage was faster than the battered rental. As damaged as Whit's car had been, she'd have been surprised if it had started up again let alone been functional enough to follow her. And even though she hadn't known exactly where she'd been going to get back to the horrible hospital, she'd found street signs that had guided her.

She bypassed the front lot to drive around the fenced-in grounds and the building to pull the borrowed Camaro into the employee lot in the back. She parked far from the gate that led to the building. If she were to be discovered, she wanted to be close to the street so no one could block the car from leaving.

Night shift must have been skeletal because there weren't that many cars in the lot. Or maybe, after her escape, some of the employees had quit for fear of getting involved in a police investigation. Maybe she should have gone to the authorities as Aaron had wanted.

But if Serenity House had influence over them, the police might have brought her right back here. Because of the holes in her memory, she didn't know if she had been legally committed to the hospital. Maybe a judge had ordered her confinement. And the authorities would have to uphold the judge's order.

That was why she'd had to go back. She couldn't stand one more minute of not knowing how she had wound up here. But she had a sick feeling that she wouldn't like what she learned. What if the king had orchestrated her disappearance?

What if he'd resented her intrusion into his life and her interference with Gabriella? He had spent years denying her existence. When she'd showed up to protect his real princess, he had agreed begrudgingly. And only because of all the attempts that had already been made to abduct the princess. Since the day she'd been brought home to the palace, Gabriella St. Pierre had been the target of kidnapping and extortion plots.

His enemies had wanted to use Gabriella for leverage—forcing King Rafael to agree to their political or business demands. And everyone else had wanted to hold the princess ransom for money because her father would have willingly paid a huge sum for her safe return.

If Charlotte had been kidnapped by mistake—which might have been the case—he wouldn't have paid a dime for her return. He would have just let her rot. Here.

Why had she wound up in a psychiatric hospital? Had it all just been a case of mistaken identity?

She turned off the car and reached into her pocket, pulling out one of the security badges she'd stolen from Aaron. Growing up with a con artist mother had had some benefits. She'd taught Charlotte to pickpocket at an early age. Not that Bonita had relied on pickpocketing to support herself. She'd just used the wallets she'd *found* to meet the men she'd wanted to meet.

Charlotte flinched with a twinge of guilt that she'd used Aaron to get what she'd wanted. Of course she'd wanted to hug him, had wanted to apologize for keeping so many secrets from him. But now that he knew his beloved Josie was alive, he wanted nothing to do with Charlotte. So when he'd pushed her away, she had pulled the badges from his pocket. She'd only intended to take one, but the lanyards had been tangled together. She had left him one…if he could get here to use it.

But dawn was already burning away the night with a low-hanging fog. Getting in now, before the day shift began, was Charlotte's best bet to go unnoticed. Because she'd been cold, she had kept on the scrubs under the warmer clothes Aaron had packed in the box for her.

He was such a considerate man—always more concerned about others than himself. It was no wonder that, even knowing his heart had already belonged to another, she'd begun to fall for him. He had reminded her of her missionary grandparents and her aunt. Always trying to save the world and uncaring of their own comfort or needs.

Her mother had been the exact opposite. And Charlotte had grown up worrying that she would become more like her than the others—since her father was also a selfish bastard. How could he have made that announcement at the ball? Cavalierly passing Gabriella from one man to another like a possession with no thoughts or feelings of her own…

Just as Charlotte had been imprisoned here—with no concern for her comfort or her feelings. She stepped out of the vehicle and peeled off the sweater and then wriggled the jeans down her legs. The exertion zapped what she had left of her strength, which had already been diminished by being restrained to a bed. And either the pregnancy or the concussion had stolen the energy she used to have.

Her legs trembled beneath her weight. Maybe she just wasn't accustomed to standing anymore. Or maybe she dreaded going back inside the hospital that had served as her prison. She tucked the stolen gun in the waistband of her pants and tugged the shirt down over it. At least now she wasn't unarmed.

But if she was caught…

She wouldn't be just tied down to that bed again. She would be taken to that airfield and whisked away on a private plane to some other prison. One from which she would probably find no escape.

And no one to help her.

If she were taken again, would Aaron even look for her this time? Or was he so angry over her lies and lies of omission that he would consider it good riddance if she went missing again?

Or would he think that she'd just taken off on her own? That she'd duped him yet again?

She glanced back toward the street, wanting to wait for him. Wanting him to come for her. But she had no way of knowing if he was coming—if he were even able or willing to come after her.

And she couldn't wait any longer. This was her last shot to find out who had abducted her—to find out the identity of the father of her baby.

"WE'RE TOO LATE," Aaron said as he pulled into the employee lot and parked beside the Camaro, which was in a space farthest from the building. Even once he'd gotten Whit's rental car started, he should have known it would never catch up to the faster vehicle Charlotte had taken. "She's probably already inside."

She must have taken the extra two badges from him when she'd hugged him. God, he'd been a fool again— to think that she'd actually been apologizing to him for all the secrets she'd kept from him.

But she'd only been playing him to get what she wanted. Access to Serenity House. After what she'd gone through—being tied down and beaten—why would she want to go back inside?

And would he be able to get her out again?

He shut off the vehicle and turned toward the three-story brick building. Lights shone in only a few windows, the rest of the rooms eerily dark.

Serenity House had been anything but serene earlier that evening—it had been like a war zone with gunfire and fighting and yelling. Hell, there had even been the vehicle knocking down the fence. But as they'd passed the front entrance, he'd seen that gate and fence had been repaired, so it appeared as though nothing had happened. And now it seemed that hardly anyone was around—guards, staff or patients.

Whit stared at the black Camaro as if trying to determine if it was the one that had raced past them earlier. "I have to admit that I'm surprised she came here at all. I figured she'd just keep driving."

"She wants to find Princess Gabriella every bit as much as you do," Aaron said. That had to be the reason she would risk going back inside. Now he understood why she'd been so protective of the princess. She hadn't been just doing her job. She'd been guarding her sister.

Whit shook his head. "I doubt that…"

"She said she doesn't want to take Princess Gabriella's place."

"She's said a lot of things."

"Actually she hasn't," Aaron said, compelled to defend her. "It wasn't that she lied to me. She just didn't tell me things."

"A lie of omission is still a lie," Whit persisted.

"I guess you'd know."

Sick of arguing with his old partner, Aaron stepped out of the car and slammed the door. "We have to find her."

Despite her skills, Charlotte needed him. She wouldn't be able to get in and out of Serenity House alone. Remembering the shots that had been fired at him earlier in this lot, Aaron moved cautiously toward the building.

Whit's footsteps followed him, the other man sticking close and keeping his voice low. "She's already beaten us to whatever we might find here."

"You don't know that." She could have been stopped at the gate. Maybe the ID badges they'd taken had been deactivated. Maybe they wouldn't open the locked gates and doors.

Disappointment and frustration made Whit's whisper gruff. "Princess Gabriella isn't here."

Aaron had already checked that out; he knew it was true. Obviously Whit had learned the same from Stanley Jessup's young reporter's source. "But maybe whoever put Charlotte here took Princess Gabriella, as well."

"I doubt both of them survived what happened in Paris," Whit replied.

"We don't know what happened in Paris."

"She does…"

Aaron was done arguing. He ignored the other man and hurried toward the gate.

"Stop," Whit ordered in a harsh whisper.

Recognizing the urgency in Whit's voice, Aaron froze and crouched lower to the pavement, wary of getting shot at again. He turned back to Whit, who was pointing toward one of the few other cars parked in the lot.

Like the fog rising up from the ground, steam covered the windows, but it didn't conceal the dark shadows of two people sitting inside the front seat.

Had Charlotte already been grabbed—before she'd even made it to the building?

With just a look and a jerk of his head, Aaron communicated with his old partner. They each took a side of the car—Whit on the driver's side and Aaron the passenger's. That was probably where Charlotte would be sitting if she were inside the vehicle.

He could only see the shadows through the fogged-up windows. He couldn't tell if the passenger was actually Charlotte. And he had no clue who the driver was. The U.S. Marshal? One of the guards?

Neither shadow moved. They must not have noticed him pass behind the vehicle on his way across the lot. Why were they just sitting there—long enough to steam up the windows?

Were they talking? Arguing?

He heard neither, nothing except for the mad pounding of his own pulse in his ears. Foreboding chilled him more than the cool gusts of wind. Something wasn't right. It had to be Charlotte…

Whit moved as silently and quickly as Aaron did. Each had his weapon clenched in his hand, the barrel glittering in the first light of dawn streaking across the sky.

Maybe he could grab her and pull her to safety before the driver even realized they were sneaking up on them. With his free hand, Aaron grabbed the handle and jerked open the door. And the passenger fell out—onto him. Blood—thick and sticky—dripped from the woman's body—saturating his shirt. And he realized it wasn't steam fogging up the windows but a spray of blood.

They were too late.

Chapter Ten

"This is why you don't want to help me," a soft voice murmured from the cover of the enveloping fog.

Startled, Aaron jerked—knocking the body off him so that it dropped onto the asphalt and rolled over. With the hole in her face from the bullet she'd taken in the back of her head, the woman was nearly unrecognizable but for the gray hair.

But she wasn't Charlotte, who stepped from the fog and approached the car.

"You're all right," Aaron said, breathing a sigh of relief that she hadn't been in the car—or entered the hospital yet.

She shook her head in denial, but he figured she was referring to her emotional state rather than her physical condition.

"It's Sandy. The nurse who took care of me," Charlotte said, identifying the woman. "She tried to help me, and look what she got for her trouble. Dead."

"Driver's dead, too," Whit informed them. He flipped open a wallet he'd taken off the body. A curse whistled between his teeth.

"What?" Aaron asked.

"It's that kid," Whit replied, "the young investigative

reporter who approached one of Stanley Jessup's editors with the story about Princess Gabriella being here."

"The nurse must have been his source," Aaron said, leaning inside the car to see that the reporter had also been shot in the back of the head like the woman.

They had probably been meeting in the parking lot to discuss what she'd witnessed that evening when someone had executed them. He suspected that their killer had been hiding in the backseat, like Whit had back at Jessup's rented cottage.

"That's why they were killed, Charlotte," he told her, trying to ease her guilt. She hadn't asked to be kidnapped and held hostage in this place. "It had nothing to do with you."

She shrugged off his reassurance. "It had everything to do with me. It wouldn't have happened if I hadn't been here. They would both still be alive."

He couldn't absolve her of guilt she was determined to hold on to—just as Whit hadn't been able to absolve him three years ago when he'd thought Josie had been murdered on their watch. The only thing that might help her was learning the truth.

"Then we need to find out who put you in here," he said, "because that's who's really responsible for these deaths."

"We don't know that," Whit said, his dark gaze narrowed with suspicion as he stared at Charlotte. Maybe he'd taken her claim of responsibility literally.

As Aaron lifted the nurse's body back into the car, he noted that her skin was already cold. "She's been dead awhile," he said. "They were probably killed shortly after Charlotte and I broke out of here. And our only lead to finding out who is behind all this is in that hospital."

He gestured back at the three-story building. But Whit continued to study Charlotte. He obviously thought she was a more viable lead. But if she knew who'd put her in this place, she would have no desire to go back inside.

Instead she drew in an audible breath and started across the lot toward the building.

He caught her arm. "You can't go back in there."

She pointed back at the car with the blood-spattered windows. "It's not any safer out here."

"She's right," Whit miraculously agreed. "We should all stick together."

Aaron figured his old partner just didn't want Charlotte getting away again before he'd had a chance to interrogate her. But, even though they didn't trust each other, maybe they would all be safer if they stayed together.

Because wasn't the saying *to keep your enemies closer...*

CHARLOTTE ACHED WITH the desire to throw her arms around Aaron's neck and cling to him. She was afraid, but her inclination had less to do with fear and more to do with relief. When she'd first realized that was blood dripping down the car windows, she'd thought that Aaron might have been inside—that he might have beaten her there using some back roads and...

Her breath hitched with a sob she held inside. She'd learned at an early age that tears were a waste of time. They had never swayed her mother from doing what she'd wanted and had never made the selfish woman care about her. She doubted crying would make Aaron care, either.

He was already in love with another woman. But

why hadn't he pressed her for Josie's whereabouts? Ironically, she was close. That was why Michigan had sounded familiar to Charlotte because she had brought Josie here for her new life.

It would be even more ironic if this was where Charlotte lost her life. But Aaron was determined to keep her safe. That was why he was still here—because it was his job. Even more than that, it was his honor. He was the kind of man who enjoyed playing white knight to helpless damsels. He was a true hero—in wartime and peace. That was why Charlotte had been so drawn to him.

But she was no damsel in distress, so she should have known that they could never be…

"Are we doing this?" Whit asked, breaking the silence that had fallen between them as she stared up at Aaron's handsome face.

His gaze was locked with hers, as if he was trying to figure out what she was thinking. Or plotting…

Aaron nodded. "Yeah, we're doing this."

"What's the plan?" Whit persisted.

"We go in the employee entrance, but we bypass the locker room and cafeteria and take the back stairs up to the administrator's office."

Whit whistled in appreciation. "You know the layout of the place."

"I interviewed here and then worked a day before I even tried getting inside her room," Aaron explained.

A grin tipped up a corner of his sexy mouth. "And then I got tossed out on my ass after I got caught coming out of her room."

"I thought you weren't coming back," she remembered with a flash of the panic she'd felt then. "I thought you'd been shot."

"Not yet," Aaron said with a glance back at the car where two people had been shot. "But we have to make this quick. Get in, get into the administrator's records, and get the hell out!"

"Good plan," Whit mused.

The first test was getting past the lock at the security gate. They all breathed a sigh of relief that a swipe of the card turned the light from red to green.

"I thought they might have deactivated them." Aaron spoke aloud the fear she'd been harboring, too. "Guess they didn't think we'd be stupid enough to come back."

But they were wrong. It probably was very stupid to return to the place they'd barely escaped the first time.

No one accosted them between the employee entrance and the stairwell to the second floor and the office suites. But the administrator's office was not empty. A light glowed behind the frosted glass in the door, and a machine buzzed inside, the floor vibrating with the low drone of it.

"She's shredding papers," Charlotte said, her stomach lurching with a sick feeling of hopelessness.

"The records are online," Aaron assured her—giving her hope as he had in the parking lot. Trying to make her feel better.

He was such a damn good man. That was why she reached for the door handle, trying to enter first. Whoever had put her in this place wanted her baby; she doubted anyone would shoot at her. But Aaron apparently wasn't willing to take that chance. He held her back, and with a nod at Whit, the two men burst through the door with their weapons drawn.

The woman standing behind the desk wore a power suit and had an air of authority—even with her ash-blond hair falling out of the bun on top of her head and dark circles blackening the skin beneath her eyes. She had to be the administrator. She confronted them with a hard stare and slight smile—more triumphant than fearful. She had definitely suspected that they would come back.

"It's too late," Dr. Mona Platt, per the nameplate on her desk, said. "I wiped the hard drive. Everything's gone…"

Charlotte shook her head. She would not be denied. She had gone too long without knowing what had happened to her. "Everything's *not* gone," she pointed out. "You're still here."

"I'm not going to tell you anything," the woman stubbornly insisted.

"You'll talk to us or the police," Aaron threatened her.

"What will I talk to the police about?" Dr. Platt asked, waving her hand over the paper shredder. "There is nothing to talk about."

Charlotte's anger flared, energizing her as her pulse raced. "You held me captive in this place!"

The woman's thin lips pursed into a tight line of defiance and denial. "I don't know what you're talking about."

"You restrained me to a bed," Charlotte accused, "and had a guard posted outside my door with a gun."

"We do not employ armed guards at Serenity House," the administrator replied prissily.

Aaron snorted at that claim.

Charlotte pointed to the bruise on her head. "Mr. Centerenian nearly killed me with that gun!"

"Mr. Centerenian was not employed by Serenity House."

"Who was he employed by?" Whit threw the question out there. "Who paid him and who paid for this woman's stay here?"

"I cannot violate doctor-patient confidentiality clauses," Dr. Platt persisted. "Or the privacy law."

"I am the patient!" Charlotte snapped. "So you're going to damn well tell me who paid you to keep me here!"

"I will not—"

Charlotte lifted her gun and pointed the barrel directly at the woman. "You will tell me!"

"You won't shoot me."

"I wouldn't be so sure of that," Whit warned the doctor. "She can't be trusted."

"And since I was confined to a psychiatric hospital, I must be out of my mind." She moved her finger to the trigger. "I could probably use an insanity plea to get out of jail time."

"Then you'd wind up spending the rest of your life in a place like this," Dr. Platt threatened.

"At least I'll be alive…"

The woman's eyes narrowed with her own temper. "You should be thanking me."

A laugh, at the woman's audacity, burst out of Charlotte's lips. "God, lady, you should be committed here yourself instead of running the place. What the hell do you think I should be thanking you for?"

Dr. Platt pointed toward Charlotte's belly. "You should thank me for your baby. You owe me for its life."

"What the hell are you talking about?" Aaron asked the question before Charlotte could.

She pressed her palm over her stomach, as if her hand alone could protect her baby from this crazy woman. "You—you did this? You impregnated me?"

The doctor shook her head, knocking more brittle

blond strands of hair loose from the bun. "I was supposed to—with special sperm. But you were already pregnant. I didn't tell *him* that, or he would have had me terminate it. You have me to thank for your baby."

"My baby…" But it wasn't just *her* baby. It was Aaron's baby, too. Even though they had used protection that one night they'd been together, it must have failed…because he was the only man she'd been with recently. In a long while, actually. She turned toward him, and when she met his gaze, she knew he *knew*.

AARON WAS GOING to be a father. The baby was *his*.

The thought stole his breath away for a moment.

Whit had no such problems. "Who is *he?*" he demanded to know.

"The father?" Dr. Platt asked with a sniffle of disinterest. "I don't know." And she obviously didn't much care. She turned toward Charlotte. "Do you remember? Or are you still suffering from amnesia?"

If the look on Charlotte's face was any indication, she knew—with as much certainty as he knew. The baby was his. But that wasn't Whit's question.

So the tenacious Mr. Howell repeated it. "Who is the man who paid you to make her pregnant with his sperm? Who brought her here?"

"That guard—the one with the gun—Mr. Centerenian is the one who brought her here," Dr. Platt replied. "And he hired a private nurse, too, who only took care of the princess."

"The princess…" Whit murmured the words.

"I am not Princess Gabriella," Charlotte replied.

The woman laughed now. "And you don't think you belong here? You've either still got amnesia or you're crazy."

"Who I am is Charlotte Green," she said, "bodyguard to Princess Gabriella."

When Dr. Platt continued to stare at Charlotte like she was crazy, Aaron said, "It's true. She's a former U.S. Marshal and professional bodyguard." The woman didn't need to know that she was also royalty. "This man—Mr. Centerenian—brought you the wrong woman. He and his boss kidnapped the wrong woman."

Dr. Platt shrugged. "It doesn't matter to me. None of these outrageous claims of yours has anything to do with me or Serenity House."

"It has everything to do with you," Aaron argued, because she was the only one who could tell them what they needed to know. "You took money to hold a woman hostage. You're an accessory."

"That man brought her here," she stubbornly repeated. "I had no idea that she had been kidnapped."

Whit swore. "Bullshit!"

"That gorilla with the gun is not the one giving the orders," Aaron said. "And he's not the one paying you. I hope his boss paid you a hell of a lot for what you're going to wind up giving up for it."

She arched a brow, her interest finally piqued. "Giving up?"

"Your hospital," Aaron said.

"Your freedom," Whit added.

"Your life," Charlotte murmured. "If I have anything to say about it…"

She didn't mean it. Aaron was almost certain that she didn't. That she was just upset. Understandably so for all she'd had to go through.

"You're threatening me," Dr. Platt accused, as if she were the victim.

Charlotte stepped closer to her, and even though she

was six months pregnant and weak, she was a far more dangerous woman than the administrator realized. "I'm not just threatening," she warned the woman.

Aaron put his hand on her arm, pulling her back before she vaulted over the desk and throttled the administrator. He told both women, "We need to know who that man is."

And if Charlotte killed Dr. Platt, they might never figure it out. Or at least be able to prove it.

"You're already in trouble here," Aaron pointed out, "so you might as well tell us what you know."

"Come on," Whit urged her.

Aaron felt them coming before he heard them. There were enough of them that there were vibrations on the floor beneath his feet. He reached for Charlotte even before the door burst open and the armed men stormed into the office. He pushed her behind him, taking cover behind a filing cabinet, and raised his weapon.

The administrator didn't have magical powers, but somehow she had summoned the guards as silently as she had last time Aaron had been in her office. Maybe she had a secret button somewhere on her desk, or maybe she had a remote alarm in her pocket.

Or maybe she hadn't summoned them at all because the first bullet they fired went through her forehead, spattering her brains on the wall behind her. There was no need to check her for a pulse; there was no way she could have survived that shot.

Then the guards swung their weapons toward them, and the office erupted with gunfire. Aaron fought hard to stay between Charlotte and the men as he returned fire. But she moved around him, taking her own shots. Aaron was so concerned about her that he hadn't even noticed that Whit was down. He'd been hit.

Aaron's heart slammed against his ribs as he noticed the blood. And in that moment of distraction, one of the guards lunged toward him with gun blazing...

Chapter Eleven

"Her guards don't have guns, my ass," Whit murmured as Aaron carried him from the building. Sirens wailed in the distance.

Charlotte's hand shook as she swiped the badge through the lock on the gate. "Maybe we should wait for the police," she said, "or at least for an ambulance."

Whit had lost a lot of blood. But that hadn't stopped him from saving her and Aaron. He'd taken out the last guard. But none of the men who had stormed into the office had been the one who'd struck her with the gun and stolen her memory. Where was Mr. Centerenian?

"We should wait for an ambulance," Aaron agreed.

Whit shook his head. "It's a through and through, and I can move my arm so it didn't hurt anything in my shoulder."

"Then you should be able to walk," Aaron grumbled, but he continued to carry his friend across the lot. And they were friends again.

Enlisting Whit to help her stage Josie Jessup's death and forbidding him to tell Aaron had destroyed their friendship. Whit had obviously resented—maybe even hated her—for it. And for three years Charlotte had regretted what her job had cost the two men. That was why she'd convinced the king to hire them both for bodyguards. She'd wanted them to work together again.

But she had never imagined how well they would have to work together. They had kept each other alive in that office, and they'd kept her alive. She wasn't certain who else had survived. Not the administrator. But some of the guards might have.

And Mr. Centerenian was out there, somewhere. So she clutched her weapon close and kept a watchful gaze on the area around them. She hoped she wouldn't have to use her gun, though, because if she had to, she would need to make the one bullet she had left count.

"Put him in Jessup's car," she ordered as she fumbled for the keys and unlocked the doors. "We need to get out of here fast."

They all squeezed into the sports car, Whit bleeding on the leather seats in the back. Charlotte passed the keys to Aaron, who drove.

"He's lost a lot of blood," she whispered, leaning across the console. Warmth radiated from Aaron, chasing some of the chill from her body. "We should take him to the hospital."

"No," Whit protested from the back. "Just take me to Stanley Jessup's. And make sure nobody follows you this time."

Aaron cursed him, but he took the route toward the lake and the house sitting high on the dune above it. "If you die, you stubborn ass," he threatened, "it's on you."

"Actually it'll be on you," Charlotte remarked with a faint chuckle as Aaron carried his friend into the house.

"I'm fine," Whit promised.

Charlotte reached for the door just as it opened, and she came face-to-face with an older man. His hair was thick and wavy and pure white despite the fact that he wasn't even out of his fifties yet. And his gaze was green and piercing. She didn't need an introduction; she knew exactly who he was. Her stomach flipped, and then the baby kicked as if in protest of Charlotte's lurch of guilt.

"What the hell happened?" the older man bellowed. "Did you shoot him, Aaron?"

Aaron chuckled. "No. Can't say I haven't been tempted, though. Where can I put him? He's all dead weight."

"I'm not dead yet," Whit weakly murmured.

"Over here," Stanley Jessup said, leading them toward a den. "Lay him down on the couch and I'll call for a private doctor."

The media mogul understood the need for discretion. Over his head, Aaron met her gaze—as if trying to convince her to tell the man about his daughter.

She was tempted. Never more so than now that she carried a child of her own. But she couldn't risk Josie's safety. Not even to ease her conscience.

"Do you need a doctor, too, your highness?" Mr. Jessup asked, his voice gruff with concern.

If only her own father had ever cared about her like a virtual stranger cared…

She shook her head at the self-pitying thought as much as in reply to his question.

"This isn't Princess Gabriella," Aaron said.

"I told you I wouldn't run the story until she got out of danger, but the story's too big…" His gaze focused on her rounded belly. "I can't sit on it anymore. The young reporter who has a source at the hospital is ready to run with his story."

Thinking of the horrific fate that had befallen that

poor kid and the nurse who had tried to help her, Charlotte sucked in a breath of pain and guilt.

"I'll call the doctor," Stanley interrupted himself. He grabbed a cell from his pocket and punched in some numbers. Then he lowered his voice as he issued commands to whoever answered his call.

"Are you all right?" Aaron asked, his focus on her rather than his bleeding friend now. "You're extremely pale."

His concern was back. But was he concerned about her or was he concerned about his child? *Of course, it's the baby.*

She was worried about the baby, too, and what could have happened with all the bullets flying. She could have easily been shot, just as Whit had. Fortunately for her—*unfortunately for Whit*—the guards had been more focused on firing at the men than at her. She suspected they'd had orders not to harm her baby. Because whoever had employed them mistakenly thought the baby was his...

The administrator had been right. But unfortunately Charlotte hadn't had the chance to thank her before the woman had been killed.

She should have listened to Aaron and stayed behind the first time he'd brought her to this house. But she hadn't wanted to be alone with Stanley Jessup almost as much as she'd wanted to learn who had kidnapped and imprisoned her in the mental hospital.

Having spent most of her professional life in dangerous situations, she hadn't had any qualms about risking her life again. After all, she had survived all those previous dangerous situations, so she'd proven that she could take care of herself.

But it wasn't just her anymore. She had someone

else to think about now—someone who wasn't a client or a witness but someone who was actually a physical part of her. Someone whose life depended on Charlotte staying alive and healthy.

As the enormity of that responsibility struck her, her knees began to shake, and she started trembling all over in reaction.

"Charlotte!" Aaron called out to her, his voice sharp with alarm. Then he repeated his earlier question, "Are you all right?"

"I—I need to sit down," she said. "Just rest for a little while, and I'll be fine." But before she could find a chair to sit on, Aaron swung her up in his arms. Black spots swam across her vision and dizziness threatened to overwhelm her. She clutched at Aaron's broad shoulders and his neck, holding on to him tightly.

"Where's a bedroom?" he asked Jessup, who'd just slipped his cell phone back in his pocket.

Even knowing that Aaron was only concerned about the baby and her health, Charlotte's pulse jumped at his question—at the idea of Aaron wanting to carry her off to a bedroom. But now that he knew how much she'd kept from him—that she'd kept Josie from him—she doubted he would ever want her—*Charlotte*—again.

Her head pounded with frustration and exhaustion, and she closed her eyes as the hopelessness washed over her. She did just need some rest—just a little—to get back her energy and her will to fight.

"Top of the stairs," the older man directed them. "There's a nice guest suite a couple of doors down the hall on the right."

She didn't care if it was nice or not. Hell, anything was nicer than Serenity House. She expected to fall asleep the minute her head hit the pillow. But when

Aaron laid her down on the bed, she tensed—unwilling to drop her arms from around his neck. She wanted to cling to him again—wanted to make sure that they had both really survived the shoot-out at Serenity House.

"After he takes care of Whit, I'll have the doctor come up to check you out," he assured her.

"You can't tell him…" she murmured as sleep tugged at her lids, bringing them down.

"I'm sure since Stanley Jessup called him, the doctor will be discreet. He won't be spreading any rumors about Princess Gabriella being pregnant."

"Gabby isn't…" Actually she didn't know that; she hadn't seen her sister in months. She had no idea how she was, and the panic must have shown on her face.

Because Aaron assured her, "Don't worry about Gabby or the doctor."

She shook her head, frustrated at his misunderstanding. "No doctor." She didn't need a doctor. She just needed sleep.

And Aaron. She needed Aaron. He was the father of her child, but she had to accept that was all he would ever be to her.

As if he couldn't stand her touch or feared she was picking his pockets again, he pulled away, albeit gently, from her grasping arms. He headed toward the door with the explanation: "I need to check on Whit. Make sure he stopped bleeding."

They had pressed a makeshift bandage, of his own handkerchief, to his shoulder, but the thin swatch of fabric hadn't done much to stem the blood loss.

So much blood…

Charlotte shuddered as she recalled the horrific crime scene they'd left. So much devastation.

Who was responsible?

"I need to talk to Mr. Jessup, too," Aaron continued with a heavy sigh.

Fighting to stay awake, she murmured, "You can't tell him about Josie..."

"It's been almost four years now," Aaron said. "What makes you think she might still be in danger?"

She placed her hands over her belly to soothe the baby's frantic kicking. Or was that her stomach churning with jealousy? And guilt churned along with that jealousy. Trigger had been telling the truth—she and Josie had become quite close. Charlotte should be worried about her friend—not Aaron.

"Trigger," she reminded him. "He wants to know where she is."

"You're sure it's her whose whereabouts he wanted to know?"

"My last case." Seeing how close Josie had been to her father had compelled Charlotte to want to get to know her own father.

It hadn't taken her long to realize that King St. Pierre would never be the father Stanley Jessup had been to his daughter. But Charlotte had stayed because of the bond she'd formed with her sister. It wasn't just outside dangers that she'd wanted to protect Gabriella from...

But now she focused on another friend. "There must be a reason Trigger wants to find Josie now. Somebody might have figured out she's alive and hired him to find out where she is."

"We haven't seen Trigger since we broke out of Serenity House," Aaron reminded her. "I don't think Josie's in danger."

"We can't be sure. Don't tell her dad."

"I won't," he promised, as he closed the blinds to shut

out the morning sun. "Don't worry. Just sleep. You're safe here. No one will hurt you."

It was too late. Someone already had. Aaron had with how easily he walked away, leaving her alone and aching for him.

Aching for a love that would never be hers...

HER LAST LUCID thought wasn't for her own safety but for someone else's. How could he have doubted—even for a minute—that her intentions weren't honorable?

Sure, he'd let Whit and all his cynicism and doubts get inside his head, but he had never considered Charlotte with his head.

He had always connected with Charlotte with his heart. That was how he'd known—no matter how morbid the crime scene in Paris was—that she wasn't dead. Because he would have known...

"She's not the princess," he told Stanley Jessup again, as he joined the older man at the bottom of the contemporary metal and glass staircase. It was a wonder he hadn't slipped carrying Charlotte up them. But then he'd been totally focused on her—on protecting her and their unborn child.

The media mogul snorted. "How big a fool do you think I am? That girl's the princess."

She was a princess. Just not the princess that Jessup thought she was.

"That girl is the princess's bodyguard," he divulged. It wasn't like it was a secret that could be kept any longer. "She had plastic surgery to look exactly like her."

Stanley Jessup whistled in appreciation of Charlotte's dedication. "Even you guys wouldn't have gone to those extremes to protect someone."

"She did." Because Princess Gabriella was her sister.

But that was a story Stanley Jessup didn't need to have because he wouldn't be able to *not* print it.

"Are you sure?"

"I've seen them both together. To people not that familiar with them, they're virtually identical." But if you really knew them, they were nothing alike.

So who had kidnapped Charlotte thinking that she was Gabriella? Someone who hadn't known either of them that well. And where was Princess Gabby?

"Doesn't matter who she is," Jessup said. "There's a hell of a story here. She was held hostage in that hospital for months, apparently. Whit got shot in that place."

Aaron glanced into the den where the doctor treated his old friend. The former war hero cursed profusely and creatively as a needle penetrated his skin, stitching up the wound.

Jessup reached for his phone again. "I'll call that young reporter and get him over here to brief us with what he knows."

Aaron shook his head. "That won't be possible."

"You need to get over this need for confidentiality," the media mogul scoffed. "There's really no such thing anymore."

"I'm not talking about the story," Aaron said. "I'm talking about the reporter. He can't come here." He swallowed hard on regret. "I'm sorry..."

The older man groaned. "I've heard that tone from you before. Heard that damn from-the-depths-of-your-soul apology. What happened?"

"I don't know for certain," he admitted. "But we found him and his source..."

"Dead?"

He nodded.

"Who did that?"

"Probably the same men who shot Whit." Four of them had stormed the administrator's office. Two had looked like the Serenity House guards he'd fought earlier—probably why they'd been so determined to shoot him. If not for Whit, Aaron might have been lying on the couch. Or in a morgue. "We left before the police arrived but we need to know what they know."

"And since you left the scene of a crime, you can't very well just waltz into the sheriff's office and ask?"

Aaron shook his head. "Only two of the men shooting at us were hospital guards." Despite Mona Platt swearing her security force was unarmed. "I don't know if the other two men worked for the hospital or someone else." Since they'd shot her first, and fatally, he heartily suspected someone else.

"The sheriff's office?"

Aaron shrugged. "We can't trust anyone." He had learned that the hard way. He couldn't even trust the woman who carried his baby. He still felt as though she had secrets, things she'd remembered but hadn't shared with him.

Gunshots echoed inside her head and blood spattered everything, blinding her with red. She shifted against the bed, fighting to awaken from the nightmare.

But it hadn't been just a dream. It was real. All of it had happened. All the death. The destruction. The senseless murders.

She could see Whit again, taking the bullet—getting knocked to the floor as blood spurted from his shoulder. But then it wasn't Whit she was seeing. It wasn't a blond man with dark eyes. Instead it was a dark-haired man with eerie light blue eyes that were wide, staring up at her in confusion as the life seeped away with the blood that pooled around him.

"Aaron!" she screamed his name, jolting awake with her heart pounding frantically with terror.

"It's okay," a deep voice murmured. And strong arms wrapped around her in the dark. "I'm here."

She clutched him close, realizing quickly that he wore no shirt. His skin was bare and damp beneath her fingers. And water trailed from his wet hair down his neck and chest. "Are you..."

Naked?

"I'm here," he assured her. He pulled her closer, so that her body pressed tightly against his. Rough denim covered his lower body. He must have only had time to pull on his jeans when he'd heard her scream.

"I thought it was you," she said, "who got shot. I thought you were dead."

"I'm fine," he said, skimming his hand over her hair—probably trying to tame the tangled mess. "How are you?"

Still trembling in reaction to her awful dream and filled with shame that she had let so many people believe their loved ones were dead. Maybe that was why she'd been so compelled to quit after Josie's case.

"Charlotte?" He eased back and tipped up her chin, his blue-eyed gaze intent on her face. "Are you all right?"

She nodded. "I'm just not quite awake yet. And it seemed so real..."

"It was real," he said. "The shooting was real. It just wasn't me."

"It was Whit," she said, remembering. "Is he okay?"

Aaron chuckled. "Sleeping off the painkillers the doctor gave him. But he'll be fine. We were lucky,"

he said, his voice gruff with emotion, "that we all survived."

"You told Mr. Jessup about the reporter?"

He nodded.

"I'm sorry." She pressed a kiss to the rough stubble
on his cheek. "I know how hard that can be…"

Even if the people she'd told hadn't always lost their
loved ones to death, they had lost them all the same.
Her lips were still on his face, but he turned his head
until they brushed across his mouth.

And he kissed her.

He knew Josie was alive, but he kissed *her.* Dare she
hope that he cared? But then he pulled back.

"We need to talk," he said, "about the baby. About
us…"

"Us?" She couldn't give in to the hope lifting the
pressure from her chest. "When you learned how many
things I'd kept from you—" *Josie* "—I didn't think
you'd be able to forgive me."

"I don't know that I have," he admitted.

And he didn't even know that she still kept one secret from him.

"I feel like you're holding something back yet," he
said.

Maybe he did know.

"Aaron…"

"But I know this isn't the right time for us to talk,"
he said. "We still don't know what happened to Princess Gabby. Or who kidnapped you. Or who shot all
those people and had us shot at…"

She had leads. Thoughts. Suspicions. But when she
opened her mouth, he pressed his fingers across her lips.

"So I don't want to talk," he said. "I want to celebrate

that we're alive." And he replaced his fingers with his mouth, kissing her deeply.

She moaned.

And he pulled away. "I'm such an idiot. You're exhausted. You've been through hell…"

"But none of that stops me from wanting you." She was surprised, though, that he wanted her since he knew that the real love of his life was still alive. But maybe he'd accepted that he couldn't be part of Josie Jessup's life without putting her in danger, so he'd decided to make do with the mother of his child.

"Charlotte…" he murmured her name with such regret.

He couldn't love her. She had to remind herself of that—so that she wouldn't fall even deeper for him than she already had.

"I shouldn't take advantage of you," he said, "like I did back at that cabin—"

She pressed her fingers over his lips now. "If anything I took advantage of you back there."

"You didn't even know who you were then."

"But I knew who you were." Strong and loyal and trustworthy. He would be a wonderful father—a far better father than she had ever known.

"I wish I knew who you are," he murmured wistfully.

"I told you—"

"I know your name," he said, "but I don't think I've ever really known you. And I'm not sure if you'll ever let me know the real you."

She didn't want him to just know her. She wanted him to love her. So she made herself vulnerable to him in a way that she never had for any other man. She didn't trust him enough to give him the words of love, but she showed him her love. With her lips and her tongue.

He lay back on the bed and groaned. He let her bring him to the brink before he turned on her. Pulling off her clothes, he kissed every inch of skin he exposed. And he pressed her back into the pillows and used his mouth to bring her beyond the brink—until pleasure tore through and she moaned his name again.

He joined their bodies, thrusting gently inside her—as if afraid that he might harm their unborn child. His slow and easy strokes drove her up again, with tension winding tight inside her. She clutched at his back, then slid her hands lower, grasping his tightly muscled butt. But he refused to rush. And each slow stroke drove her a little crazier—until she just dissolved with pleasure and emotion.

Then he groaned and filled her. "Charlotte…"

She was the woman whose name he uttered when pleasure overwhelmed him. She wanted to hope it meant something—that it might indicate they could have a future. But she had had her hopes dashed too many times to entertain any now. He flopped onto his back beside her and curled her against his side. But she couldn't look at him—couldn't let him see how much she cared. So she gazed around the room. The curtains were still drawn tight over the blinds—shutting out whatever light might be outside. "How long did I sleep?"

"Probably not long enough," he said. "You were exhausted. I should have let you go back to sleep instead of…"

"I must have spent months in that bed in Serenity House," she reminded him. "I shouldn't ever be tired again."

"But, even before what we just did, we had quite a night," he pointed out. "A night we were damn lucky to have survived."

And that was the only reason they had made love—in celebration of that survival, and for a wonderful while, she had been able to replace the pain and fear with pleasure. But now it all came rushing back along with her nightmarish memories of the night.

Her breath shuddered out in a ragged sigh as she remembered it all. "That was just one night? You got caught in my room and then came back to break me out all in the same night?"

"Yes."

Now she remembered something else—the guard's phone call. "Mr. Centerenian's boss is coming here tonight—to some private airfield. The guy who kidnapped and tried to impregnate me is going to be here."

"The guy who thought he was kidnapping and impregnating Princess Gabriella," Aaron pointed out. "This has nothing to do with you."

"She's my sister," Charlotte said with pride. "It has everything to do with me." It was her responsibility to keep the real princess safe.

Aaron shook his head. "I'll take it from here. I'll figure out which airfield they'll be using, and I'll meet him there."

"You're not going alone."

She didn't want to risk the baby's safety again, but she didn't want the baby's father putting his life at risk without backup he could trust, either.

"Absolutely not," he said. "I will not let you put yourself and my baby in danger again."

Chapter Twelve

Aaron momentarily took his gaze from the airfield to glance at the woman sitting in the passenger seat. She had come along. While he had admitted to himself and to Whit that he didn't know her as well as he should, he was already intimately familiar with her stubbornness.

If he had forbidden her to join him, she would have stolen another car from the garage and tracked down the airfield on her own. At least now, going together, it would be easier for him to protect her.

But she hadn't come along thinking that he would keep her safe. If anything she might think she needed to protect him...

But more likely she didn't trust him to tell her what he discovered on his own. And she wanted to know who'd locked her up in a psychiatric hospital. But what were all her motives? To keep Gabriella safe? They didn't even know where she was. Or so that Charlotte could take revenge on the person who had stolen nearly six months of her life?

Studying the dark airfield through the car windows, Aaron wasn't certain they would discover anything. They had been parked outside it since night had first begun to fall, and there were no lights illuminating the

single runway or the steel hangar beside it. There was
no vehicle parked near the hangar, either. They had
parked Stanley Jessup's car on a farmer's access road
to his fields that surrounded the small, private airport.

"This place looks deserted," he mused aloud.

He had no more than uttered the words when lights
flashed on—bright beams of light pointing up into the
night sky—to guide a plane to ground.

"He was here—that guard from the hospital—he's
been here the whole time," Aaron said with a glance at
Charlotte. "You knew it?"

She nodded.

"But there's no car anywhere around here…" So
they'd shut off the Camaro's lights and waited in the
dark for him to drive up.

"You said it's the only private airfield in the area,"
she reminded him. "He's here…"

Aaron nodded with sudden realization of how they'd
missed him. "He must have parked his car inside the
hangar."

Charlotte reached for the door handle. "We need to
get inside there, too."

Aaron grabbed her arm, stopping her from stepping
out. "No. *We* don't."

"We can't let him get on that plane and just fly away,"
she said. "He's the only lead we have left."

The reporter was dead. The nurse. The administrator.
And if any of the armed men from the office had survived, they weren't talking yet. Stanley Jessup had developed a source in the sheriff's office. The small town
was overwhelmed and bringing in state and federal authorities to take over the investigation. While that would
be better for him and Whit and Charlotte, it would take
too long for the investigation to yield any results.

"I will go," he clarified. "You will stay here."

"So he can sneak up on me, grab me and force me onto the plane?" She shuddered at the thought.

"You're armed," he reminded her. "I doubt he could force you to do anything." And that was part of the reason he'd agreed to let her come along with him. She really could take care of herself.

So was she more worried about him? That he'd take a bullet without her being there to protect him? Maybe she had feelings for him, too. Or was she just trying to keep alive the father of her baby?

"We decided to stick together," she reminded him. "That's what kept us alive in the administrator's office—sticking together."

"Glad Whit didn't hear you say that." They'd snuck out of the house while the other man had still been sleeping off his painkillers. Hopefully they would be back before he ever woke up.

Her lips curved into a faint smile. "He's in no condition to be here with us."

Aaron pressed his palm over her stomach. "Neither are you."

"I'm pregnant," she said. Then she dragged in a shaky breath and repeated, "I'm pregnant." She expelled the breath and said, "I'm not sick or injured."

Now he moved his hand to the bruise on her temple. "You were hurt," he pointed out the yet to heal injury. Thinking of the pain she'd endured, the fear over her lost memory and months of imprisonment, his stomach clenched as if he'd been punched in the gut again. "And you're lucky to be alive."

"I am alive," she said.

But what about Gabriella? Learning her fate was

probably what compelled Charlotte to put herself at risk again.

"And now I remember who I am," she added. "And I know what I know—how to take care of myself."

"And others…" He patted her belly again and nodded. "Let's get in there while the plane's landing." When the guard was distracted with the plane, they would be able to get the jump on him.

CHARLOTTE WINCED AT every snap of twig and rustle of grass beneath their feet as they moved stealthily toward the hangar. It was so damn quiet, and so damn black but for those lights beaming into the sky. She stumbled in the dark, would have tripped and gone down, but for Aaron catching her arm and steadying her.

She waited for him to use her clumsiness as a reason to insist on her returning to the car. But instead he kept his hand on her, keeping her close to his side.

Heat and attraction radiated between them. He may not trust her. Hell, he may not ever be able to forgive her, but he did want her. He'd proven that back at the house—proven it in a way that had her still feeling boneless and satiated.

The man was an amazing lover. If only he could really love her—*deeply* love her…

She shook off the wistful thought. It must have been the hormones—due to the pregnancy—that had her hoping for things she knew weren't possible. She had never been the romantic type.

She had always been a pragmatic person. She knew how the world really worked—her mother had made certain of that.

Now she had to make certain that the threat against

Princess Gabriella was gone. She clasped her weapon tightly in her hand.

Aaron reached for the handle to the back door of the steel hangar. He tested the lock and nodded.

The idiot guard wasn't as careful here as he'd been at the hospital. Mr. Centerenian would have never left the door to her room unlocked.

Charlotte lifted her weapon and nodded that she was ready. Aaron opened the door and stepped inside first, keeping his body between her and whoever might be in the hangar. Like her, he probably doubted that there was only one man meeting the plane—after all the men who had stormed into the administrator's office.

But the hangar was quiet and filled with light from the door open onto the field. One man stood there, staring up at the sky. A cigarette tip glowed between the fingers of his left hand. A white bandage swaddled his right hand.

"It's him," she whispered.

The man tensed and dropped his cigarette. Then he reached for the gun in the holster beneath his jacket. Before he could withdraw it, the drone of an engine broke the quiet. Mr. Centerenian turned his attention to the lights in the sky.

The plane was coming. The plane that Charlotte was supposed to leave on—to God knew where. A brief moment of panic clutched her heart. But she reminded herself that she wasn't going to be leaving—at least not on anyone's terms but hers.

As the guard stepped outside the hangar to watch the plane begin its descent, they moved through the shadows and edged closer to that wide-open door. But Charlotte clutched Aaron's arm—holding him back from going any farther. They ducked down below the side of the black SUV parked inside the hangar—keeping it between them and the guard.

She held tightly to Aaron's arm, making sure he stayed down. They couldn't be detected before the plane landed, or the guard might wave it off. And then they might never learn who had orchestrated her kidnapping. She had to know…

Her heart beat with each second that passed before the tires touched down on the airstrip. Calling it such was generous. It was obviously used mostly for crop dusting—not private planes coming from foreign countries. That had to be where Mr. Centerenian's boss came from. Was it someone working for her father? Dread welled up inside her at the thought. The plane bumped along the rough runway before finally coming to a stop.

The engine wasn't killed though; it continued to drone on even as the door lifted on the side. "Get her!" a voice yelled from inside the plane. "We can't stay here."

"I—I can't get her," Mr. Centerenian yelled from the entrance to the hangar. Obviously he was afraid of being too close to his boss when he gave him the bad news. "She got away."

"You lost her?"

He shook his head in denial of any culpability. "No. She got away from the hospital. She escaped."

"You were there so that would not happen," the boss reminded him—his voice terse with anger and frustration. "You need to find her! Now!"

"What are they saying?" Aaron asked, his breath warm as he whispered in her ear.

She shivered. "They're talking about me." And until he'd asked, she hadn't even realized the men had been speaking another language. Charlotte had been multilingual since a very young age.

Her grandparents had been missionaries. Whenever Charlotte had gotten in the way of her mother's latest scam, she'd been left with her grandparents—in whichever country they were working in—trying to take care of starving children and orphans.

Her mother had resented their concern for other children—had resented that they'd spent all their time and money trying to take care of everyone else in the world. At least her aunt had understood, and after her grandparents died, Aunt Lydia had taken over their good work.

And in her own way, Charlotte had thought she was honoring her grandparents, too—by taking care of people in trouble, by protecting them like they'd wanted to protect all those underprivileged children.

The plane engine cut out. "We are not leaving here until we find her," the man ordered the guard. He stomped down the steps to the ground. He wore a silk suit, and his hair was as oily and slicked back as the creepy guard who worked for him.

A breath whistled between Aaron's teeth as he recognized the guy the same time Charlotte did. Prince Linus Demetrios had been promised Princess Gabriella's hand in marriage. They had been betrothed since the day she'd been born—until the king had rescinded that promise. The day of the ball at the palace—the night she and Aaron had made love—the king had promised Gabriella to another man, a wealthier, more influential prince from another neighboring country.

And sometime during that night, someone had slipped a note under Gabby's door that she would die before she would ever marry Prince Tonio Malamatos. That was why Charlotte had whisked them off to Paris the next morning—under the ruse of meeting with designers to begin work on the princess's wedding gown.

"She could be anywhere," the guard protested. "Surely she must have contacted the authorities by now. They'll be looking for us!"

"Princess Gabriella is mine," the prince said. "We're not leaving without her and my baby."

Despite Aaron's arm on her shoulder, trying to hold her down, Charlotte jumped up. "This baby is not yours!"

"Gabby!" The prince hurried forward, his arms outstretched as if to hug her close.

She lifted the gun and pointed it directly at his chest. He had to be the one who'd threatened her sister as well as kidnapping Charlotte. "I am not Gabby, either."

"Yes," the prince insisted. "You are my sweet, sweet Gabriella."

She shook her head. "'Fraid not."

"She kept saying that," the guard related. "Kept saying that we'd grabbed the wrong woman."

Prince Demetrios shook his head, but his swarthy complexion paled in the bright lights of the airstrip. "No. That's not possible."

"I'm Charlotte Green," she said. "You know that—now that you see me."

His voice lacked conviction even as he continued to insist, "It can't be..."

"You've seen us together," she reminded him, "at the ball." Because Gabriella had thought she could trust him. As well as being engaged since birth, they had been friends that long, too. She'd felt horrible over what her father had done.

One of his heavily lidded eyes twitched as anger

overwhelmed him. "I prefer not to remember that night and all its betrayals."

Now she wanted to calm him down, to make him see reason. If he hadn't kidnapped her, she might have almost felt sorry for him. In one night he'd lost the life he'd known—the one he'd planned—just like she had when she'd lost her memory. "Gabby and I had nothing to do with the king changing his plans."

"Suddenly my country—my wealth—was not sufficient for his daughter," the prince griped with all wounded pride. "For you..."

"I am not Gabriella," she said again, her voice sharp with irritation. "I am her bodyguard." And her sister. "You know we look exactly alike. I had plastic surgery to look like her, so that I could protect her from situations like this, from her getting abducted."

"Where is she?" Aaron asked the question. "What have you done with her? You must have mistaken her for Charlotte. Did you kill her?"

"Of course not! I would never kill anyone," he protested. "That was not part of the plan."

"What was the plan?" Aaron asked. "To kidnap and rape a woman?"

That eyelid twitched again. "I would never harm the woman I love. I was helping her. Her father put her in an impossible situation, and I gave her a way out. Since she's carrying my baby, the king cannot possibly make her marry another man."

"She's not carrying your baby," Aaron said. "She's carrying mine."

The prince sucked in a breath of outraged pride. "That is not possible."

"She was already pregnant when you grabbed her in Paris," Aaron explained. "She's carrying my baby."

Charlotte's heart warmed with the possessiveness in Aaron's voice. He had claimed her baby. If only he would now claim her...

"It doesn't matter whose baby I'm carrying," she said. "I'm not Gabriella."

The prince turned toward his guard. "Could it be? Did you grab the wrong woman in Paris?"

The guard shook his head. "There was only one woman in that suite."

ONLY ONE WOMAN. Aaron couldn't even consider the implications of that claim. "There was so much blood, so much destruction," he said. "The authorities believe someone died there."

The guard nodded. "I lost a friend because of this woman. I could not hurt her then...because I had my orders to not harm the princess." He lifted the gun he clutched in his nonbandaged hand. "But if she's really not the princess..."

"I'm not," she said, "but I am the woman holding a gun on your boss. And I'm not so sure that you're going to be all that accurate shooting with your left hand. So if your bullet misses, mine won't."

The prince shuddered at her cold pronouncement and so did Aaron. She would have no qualms about pulling that trigger—about taking the life of an unarmed man.

"You're not my sweet Gabriella," the prince said, his voice choked with disappointment. "Where is she?"

"Where you will never get to her," Charlotte vowed with a conviction that had disappointment clenching Aaron's heart in a tight fist.

He realized that she had known all along—or at least as soon as her memory returned—exactly where Princess Gabriella was. Obviously because she had stashed her there...

Charlotte pushed the barrel of her gun against the prince's skinny chest. "You're going to be locked up for the rest of your life."

Maybe she didn't know—maybe that was simply what she meant—that he wouldn't be able to get to Gabriella through the prison bars he would be behind.

"I told you that I harmed no one," Prince Demetrios insisted.

"You were the one who killed my friend," the guard said, clutching that gun tightly. The murderous intent in his eyes revealed how much he wanted to pull that trigger, how much he wanted to take Charlotte's life— after having already taken her freedom and her memory.

"There are a stack of bodies back at Serenity House," Aaron said, "thanks to you."

The prince turned toward his employee. "Mr. Centerenian? What are they talking about?"

The guard tensed. With guilt? But he claimed, "I have killed no one...*yet*."

"That nurse was killed." Charlotte addressed the prince instead of his employee. "The one you hired to take care of me. Sandy..."

"And the young reporter the nurse tipped off about your kidnapping," Aaron added. "And the administrator you paid to impregnate the princess with your sperm."

"She didn't do it," Charlotte hastened to add when the prince's dark gaze lowered to her stomach. "Is that why you ordered her and the others killed? To cover your tracks?"

"Bullets were flying everywhere," Aaron said. "It was a wonder that Charlotte wasn't hit, too." Or him. It was bad enough that Whit had been.

The prince shook his head—his pride appearing every bit as wounded as it had over losing his fiancée. "I am not a killer," he said.

"You didn't pull the trigger yourself," Charlotte agreed.

"But you must have had your goon do it," Aaron finished for her.

The prince glanced toward his guard again. Even he must have begun to suspect him. "I told you to take her and to keep her safe."

Aaron gestured toward the bruise on her head. "He did that to her. He nearly killed her—despite your orders. You don't think he could have hurt anyone else?"

The prince glared at his employee. "I did not tell you to kill anyone."

"You are a fool," the guard remarked with pure disgust. "You will spend the rest of your life in prison. You do not understand that you can't leave loose ends."

"So you shot them?" Charlotte asked. "You killed all those people."

"The reporter and that stupid nurse," the guard agreed. "And now all of you. I will not spend my life in prison for some lovesick fool."

And he raised his gun and fired.

Chapter Thirteen

"Nice shot," Charlotte remarked, as the guard clasped his other hand. Aaron had used a bullet to knock the gun from the guard's hand.

But the man didn't stop—he charged at Aaron and tackled him to the cement floor of the hangar. His breath audibly whooshed out of his probably almost crushed lungs. Mr. Centerenian was much larger than Aaron but more fat than muscle. Aaron was the more experienced fighter. He tossed him off with a kick and a punch. Then the guard swung back. But Mr. Centerenian screamed in pain when his bloodied fist connected with the cement floor since Aaron had rolled out of his line of fire.

The two men continued to grapple with each other. But another man made his move, stepping back from Charlotte and heading toward the plane.

She caught him by the back of his jacket. "You're not going anywhere...except behind bars."

The tall man turned slowly toward her. Then he moved, as if to lunge at her.

But she lifted her gun and pressed it into his chest again. "I told you that I will shoot you," she said. "Given what I went through—the months I lost—because of you, I really should kill you."

"I thought you were Gabriella…"

"And that makes me want to pull this trigger even more," she said. Anger and dread surged through her with the thought of Gabby enduring what she had. The pain. The confusion.

First her father had betrayed the princess. And now the man she had considered a lifelong friend had betrayed her, too. Despite Gabby having grown up with the palace and the money, Charlotte was really more fortunate; she had learned early to count on no one. To trust no one.

She'd also learned that it was safer to love no one. But she'd messed up there. First she'd fallen under the spell of her sister's sweetness. And then Aaron's irresistible charms…

"Is she all right? Is she safe?" Prince Demetrios asked, his pride forgotten as he pleaded for information.

Gabby had considered him a friend when it seemed obvious now that he'd been more of a stalker.

"I need to know," he asked, his voice cracking with emotion. "I have loved her my whole life. I need to know that she's all right."

Whatever sympathy she'd fleetingly felt for the man was gone. She cared only about making sure Gabby was safe now. "And I need to know everything you know. I need to know every damn thing that you were behind."

"I told you," the prince said, his voice rising so that he sounded more like a whiny child than a grown man. The king had been right to end this betrothal—for so many reasons. "I only wanted Gabby—wanted us bound together for life."

"And instead so many people lost their lives," she mused and glared at him with condemnation.

"I didn't know that Mr. Centerenian shot the nurse and a reporter."

"And the administrator," Charlotte added.

"And my friend." Aaron jerked the beaten guard to his feet and shoved him toward the prince. "Make him tell us everything."

"I did," Mr. Centerenian insisted. "I told you that I cleaned up the mess he left. I killed the nurse and the man she kept sneaking away to meet. I did not kill anyone else."

"Then you hired those men to kill the administrator," Aaron said. "And try to kill us."

"No," the guard protested. "I knew Dr. Platt would not talk. And she had promised to get rid of any evidence that could lead back to the prince or me."

"Someone killed her," Aaron said. "So you didn't need to worry about that evidence after all. Or about her testifying against you."

"I told you—she would not talk."

Charlotte believed that—the woman had seemed quite stubborn. But she'd obviously had her price. Prince Demetrios had found it; someone else might have been able—if they'd had deep enough pockets. "I don't know about that. But I do know that, with all those bullets flying in that office—" she patted her stomach "—we could have been killed, too."

The prince gasped in horror. He was a sick man. But apparently he was not a killer.

"I had orders to not harm you," Mr. Centerenian said, "or I would not have been paid."

She touched the bruise on her temple now.

"Kill you," he amended himself. "I could not kill you. But had I known who you really were…"

She would have been dead. But even with all those bullets flying, none had come close to her. Maybe the shooters had just had qualms about killing a pregnant woman. Or maybe they'd had orders. At any rate, she believed someone other than Mr. Centerenian and Prince Demetrios had hired them.

Why?

"WHAT ABOUT THE parking lot?" Aaron asked the guard as an officer loaded him into the backseat of a state police cruiser.

He had called the authorities from the phone they'd found in the hangar. And the only reason he and Charlotte weren't being loaded into cruisers themselves for questioning was because of the threats of Stanley Jessup's influential lawyer. They had called the media mogul, too.

The older man had gone above and beyond all the favors Aaron had asked of him. Well, except for telling Whit where he was. But he had only confided in the other man because Whit had convinced him that Aaron was in danger.

Stanley Jessup was a hell of a lot more forgiving than he would have been. If someone had failed to protect his daughter, Aaron wouldn't have cared if the guy put himself in danger. Hell, he would have preferred it. Instead Stanley kept helping them—with doctors, lawyers and a safe place to stay.

But no place would ever be really safe if there was another shooter out there.

He asked the guard again, "You shot at me in the parking lot, right?"

Mr. Centerenian shook his head and then boasted, "I would not have missed had I been shooting at you."

Aaron could have pointed out that he had missed him in the hall. That he'd hit a vase instead of him. But this man didn't matter anymore. He apparently wasn't behind the shooting in the administrator's office.

So who was?

The prince was being loaded into the back of a separate police cruiser. Charlotte stood beside him, facing the prince instead of Aaron.

"You said that you'd tell me where Gabriella is," the prince implored her. "We had a deal…"

"The deal was," she corrected him, "that you would tell me everything you know—"

"And I did," he interjected.

"And I would tell you that she was all right—not where she is," Charlotte reminded him of the details of their agreement. "She's all right."

"But you won't tell me where she is?"

She shook her head, and the long waves of golden-brown hair rippled down her back. "I won't tell anyone where she is."

But she knew. Aaron heard the certainty in her voice. All this time he and Whit had been concerned about Princess Gabriella and Charlotte had known exactly where she was.

Whit was right. Again. When was he going to learn that he couldn't trust Charlotte Green?

"Don't ask me," she said as she stood beside him, watching the police cars leave the airstrip.

"I know better than to think you'd tell me anything," Aaron admitted. "But you should tell the king. He's been out of his mind worrying about her."

"Of course he has."

Aaron winced at his insensitive remark. "I'm sure he's been worried about you, too," he amended himself. "It's just that I didn't know then that you're his—"

"Bastard?" She shrugged, as if she didn't care, but he suspected she cared a lot. "Doesn't matter. I don't matter. Only the legitimate heir matters. Gabriella is the only child he can profit from—using her to further his empire with money and power. That's why I won't tell him where she is."

"But aren't you using her, too, then?" Aaron pointed out her double standard. "To get back at him for never acknowledging you?"

Her eyes, the same golden-brown of her hair, darkened with anger. "I wouldn't use Gabby. I only want to keep her safe."

"Is she?" Aaron wondered. "We don't know who's behind the shooting in the administrator's office."

"If we believe Mr. Centerenian and the prince's claims that it wasn't one of them," she said.

"We shouldn't," Aaron agreed. "We shouldn't believe or trust anyone." That fact had been driven home to him time and time again—with every lie and omission Charlotte had uttered.

Charlotte nodded. "And that's why I won't tell the king where Gabby is."

"That's the reason you're telling yourself," Aaron agreed. "To justify not telling him. But we both know that's not the real reason."

"Let's forget about my reasons," she said, "and focus on the reason that someone would have been shooting at you in the parking lot—"

"So I wouldn't be able to come back for you," he pointed out. That was what he'd figured at the time. Now he wasn't so certain...

"The guard said he didn't do it."

"And we trust what he said?"

She shrugged. "He admitted to two murders. Why wouldn't he admit to trying to kill you? What difference would it make at this point?"

"It would answer the rest of our damn questions," he said. "Well, not all of our questions."

Because she refused to tell him where Princess Gabriella was...

"If we figure this out, if I'm sure she's safe," Charlotte said, "I will consider revealing her location."

He nodded. "So we'll figure this out. If not the guard, who else would want to shoot at me?"

"And Whit," she said. "He was hit in the administrator's office."

"You were shot at, too," he reminded her.

"You stood between me and gunmen, kept me behind the filing cabinet," she said. "So no one really shot at me." But she had shot back.

If she hadn't, he and Whit probably wouldn't have made it out of that office alive. They probably would have wound up as dead as the administrator had.

"Just because you didn't get shot, doesn't mean you weren't the target," he pointed out. "But if you weren't, the shooting seems like more work of the prince."

Or was there someone else out there that Aaron had been too naive to consider? Just like he had been naive to think that Charlotte had finally started being honest with him.

"What about Trigger?" she asked. "Where has he been since he dropped us at that cabin?"

"Maybe the guard got rid of him like he had the reporter and the nurse," Aaron said. But then why wouldn't he have admitted it as he'd admitted to the other two murders?

Charlotte shook her head. "I doubt it. Trigger is like a cat with nine lives. He's out there. Somewhere."

CHARLOTTE SHUDDERED AT the thought. She hadn't liked working with the older man. Mostly because he had been a first-class jerk and a male chauvinist. But also because she hadn't trusted him.

Trigger had reminded her too much of her mother—both were totally concerned with their own welfare and no one else's.

If he'd ever had a daughter, he would have sold her, too. She'd suspected he would have sold a witness's location, and that was why she hadn't told him where Josie Jessup had been relocated.

She had only told one person where Josie was—just in case something ever happened to her. And she'd thought the two women would be good friends.

Had Trigger figured that out? Had he figured out where she'd stashed Gabriella? And if they'd convinced the man that she was Gabriella, then he would think that Gabriella was Charlotte Green, his ex-partner.

"I have a bad feeling," she said.

"You're not feeling well?" Aaron asked, reaching for her arm to steady her. "We should get you back to the house."

He led her toward the car and helped her into the passenger's seat.

No matter how angry he was at her—and she suspected he was furious since she hadn't told him she knew where Princess Gabby was—he was still courteous with her. Because of the baby?

"I may have put Gabby at risk," she admitted, hating herself for what she'd done. "And not just Gabby but Josie, too."

"What have you done?" he asked.

"I told Gabby where Josie is," she admitted. "If Trigger finds her..." He wasn't beyond torturing her to discover where the witness was hidden—especially not if he was being paid handsomely to find her.

"You're the only one who knows where Gabby is," he said.

Now she couldn't tell him what she had done. Aaron would probably never forgive her for putting the life of the woman he loved in danger. And she knew better than to reveal a witness's location to anyone. But she had never felt closer to another human being than she had her sister.

Until now.

To soothe herself more than her baby, she rubbed her hands over her belly. Aaron had given her this child, but yet she didn't feel as close to him. Because one woman—a woman she herself considered a friend—had always stood between them.

"Josie's fine," Aaron said. "She's safe."

His empty assurances hung in the air between them as he drove the distance back to Stanley Jessup's rental house. He pulled the car up next to the dark house and turned off the engine. "We'll ask Whit to help us get to the bottom of who is behind the other shootings."

After his taking a bullet for Aaron back in the administrator's office, she now trusted the king's other bodyguard—as much as she let herself trust anyone. But would Gabriella?

The man had hurt her...because he had let her go. He had just stood there, the morning after the ball, and had silently watched her leave for Paris, to design her wedding gown to marry another man. Like Charlotte with Aaron, Gabriella had hoped for more with Whit Howell.

"I'm not sure we should include Whit," she said, remembering that Gabby had claimed to want nothing more to do with him.

"The doctor said the bullet didn't strike anything vital," Aaron assured her. "Once the painkillers wear off, he'll be fine—determined to go again."

"But maybe he shouldn't…"

He studied her face in the darkness. "You still don't trust Whit?"

She held her breath, unwilling to admit her real problem with Howell—sisterly allegiance.

"You trusted him enough to involve him in faking Josie's death."

And not Aaron. She needed no further assurance that he would never get over not knowing that Josie hadn't really died.

"I can understand you not trusting me back then," Aaron said, surprising her with his words and his closeness as he leaned across the console separating their seats. "You didn't know me that well."

She hadn't known Whit then either, so she'd trusted Josie's judgment on which one of her bodyguards to include in her plan. Josie hadn't wanted to put Aaron in the untenable position of having to lie to her father. She'd said he was too nice to have to deal with that burden. They hadn't realized that they'd given him a far heavier burden of guilt to carry in thinking that he'd failed to protect Josie.

"But you know me now, Charlotte." His hands covered hers on her belly, and he entwined their fingers, binding them together just as their baby did. But then he leaned even closer, and his lips brushed over hers with teasing, whisper-soft kisses.

Her breath caught in her throat as desire overwhelmed her. The man's kisses stole away her common sense as effectively as that blow to her head had stolen her memories. All he had to do was touch her and she wanted him, the need spiraling out of control inside her.

But it was more than want. More even than need. It was love.

Aaron pulled back and asked, "So why do you still not trust me?"

Because he could hurt her more than anyone else ever had. Because she wanted more from him. She wanted his love. But he wasn't talking about their relationship.

"I get why you didn't tell me about Josie," he said. "But you should have told me about Gabriella." He stepped out of the car and slammed the door behind himself.

Gunshots echoed the slam. The windows burst, glass shattering as bullets hit them.

Shards struck Charlotte, stinging her skin, but she didn't duck yet. Because she was looking for Aaron. He'd disappeared. Had he been hit?

Her door creaked open, and a strong hand grasped her arm, pulling her from the car. Just like Paris, she was getting grabbed again. And just like Paris, she wouldn't go without a fight.

Chapter Fourteen

Aaron grunted as her elbow struck his chin. "Stop it," he said. "I'm trying to help you."

It was probably too late for him to help Whit. He couldn't believe he hadn't realized it before. He should have known...

Charlotte gasped in shock, and her struggles ceased. "You're all right?"

He nodded, his chin rubbing against her silky soft hair. Physically he was fine. For the moment...

"Trigger must have followed us," she said, whispering since the gunshots had stopped. "He must have found this place."

"I'm not so sure it's Trigger." He had a horrible feeling that it was someone else.

She peered around the car, looking for the shooter. "Who else...?"

"Maybe a man who lost his daughter..."

"The king?" She shook her head in rejection of that idea. "Rafael doesn't care enough about either me or Gabriella to—" She gasped and turned to him with wide eyes. "Josie's father?"

"I was a fool to ask for his help," Aaron said. "It must

have brought all those feelings rushing back—all his pain and resentment."

"No…" She shook her head, her brow furrowing with confusion. "It doesn't make any sense…"

"Stanley Jessup gave me the tip that brought me here," he reminded her. Sure, Aaron had asked the man to flush out any leads to Princess Gabriella's whereabouts. And in doing that, he might have given the grieving father the perfect opportunity to take his revenge.

Charlotte expelled an unsteady breath. "And he came, too."

"And more than that, he told Whit that I was here—getting us both in the same place." Another gunshot rang out, pinging off the metal roof of the sports car. "It has to be Jessup."

Charlotte shook her head. "No, it has to be someone else." She ducked low as shots pinged off the fenders. "Josie talks about her dad all the time." Her voice carried a faint trace of wistfulness. "She told me what a good man he is…"

"Josie was the center of his universe," Aaron said. "She meant everything to him." His baby wasn't even born, and he could identify with those feelings. Maybe because he already had those feelings for Charlotte. If something had happened to her…

She clutched her gun in her hand, but she seemed reluctant to aim it in the direction from which the shots had come. Maybe she was reluctant to take a shot and hurt a man who had already been through so much pain. "But I didn't think he blamed you two for what happened—or what he thinks happened to Josie."

"I blamed us," Aaron reminded her. "I ended my partnership—my friendship—with Whit."

For no reason. Whit had only been doing his duty—keeping Josie safe. And now Aaron might never have the chance to regain the friendship he had stupidly and stubbornly given up.

"I have to get in that house," he said, fear and desperation clawing at him as it had when he'd stood outside that burning house over three years ago and thought he'd been too late to save Josie. "I have to make sure that Whit—that Whit is…"

She must have picked up on his hopelessness because she squeezed his arm reassuringly. "Whit Howell is resourceful," she reminded him. "And he's smart. Maybe he figured it out in time."

"Whit was out," Aaron said, and he hated himself for really doing what he'd thought he and Whit had done three years ago—leaving someone alone and vulnerable who had needed his protection. While he hadn't actually failed Josie, he had failed his friend—the man who'd risked his life to save Aaron's more than once. "He was out cold on those painkillers—a sitting duck for Stanley Jessup to take his revenge."

The gunfire continued to come, bullets striking the car and the asphalt driveway near them. "But why is he shooting at *me*?" Charlotte asked. "Do you think Whit told him how I was involved?"

"No." He shook his head. "If he knew his daughter was still alive, he wouldn't be shooting at all," he told her. "Maybe he's using you to try to flush me out."

Or maybe Jessup intended to take Aaron's family from him the way that he thought his family had been taken from him.

"Let's flush *him* out," Charlotte suggested, raising her gun. "You need to get in that house. You need to check on Whit." Even though she hadn't always seemed to trust his friend and vice versa, she was concerned about him—enough to risk her own safety. She rose up and fired off a round of shots in rapid succession, giving Aaron the time and the cover to sprint toward the house.

Keeping low, he ran toward the windows of the den and, heedless of the glass, jumped through them. A hard fist struck his jaw, knocking him down onto the floor. He hit the hardwood with a bounce and popped up again to strike back. He swung his gun like a bat, hitting out with the handle. Blindly—because he couldn't see anything but a big shadow in the total darkness.

The man's eyes must have adjusted better to the dark because he caught Aaron's weapon and tried to wrest it from his grasp. Aaron was stronger, though, and retained control of the gun. He twisted it around and pressed the barrel against the temple of the man.

"Just shoot me then, you son of a bitch," the guy said with a snarl of rage and hatred.

Aaron uttered a deep laugh of pure relief. "You're alive!"

"Yeah," Whit grumbled, almost as if he wasn't entirely convinced that he lived yet. "But I feel like crap from the painkillers, and then I get attacked. By you..."

"I didn't think it was you," Aaron explained. "I thought you got shot again."

"The gunman's out there," Whit said, as more gunfire shattered the night. His voice dropped with suspicion. "Where's Charlotte?"

"She's not the shooter." But he'd left her alone with him. Panic clutched Aaron's stomach. "She's out there. She covered me, so I could get in here to check on you."

Whit snorted. "So you both thought I was dead? Some confidence—"

He grabbed Whit, inadvertently clutching his bad

shoulder and eliciting a cry of pain from his friend. But he didn't have time to apologize—not with Charlotte out there alone. "Where's Stanley?"

"He went down to the police station to help you out," Whit said. "He thought you guys might get booked no matter what his lawyer said to the authorities."

"Are you sure he really left?" Aaron asked. "You weren't still out of it?"

Whit shook his head. "No. I was clearheaded—even offered to go with him, but he said no."

"He wanted you here," Aaron said, "so that he could take his revenge on us together."

Whit snorted again. "Revenge?"

"Because of Josie."

Whit lifted a hand to his head, as if trying to clear it of the aftereffects of the painkillers. "But Josie's not dead."

"Her father doesn't know that," Aaron pointed out. "He thinks she's dead and he probably blames us. He hired us to protect her, and we failed."

Whit opened his mouth again but only a groan escaped. And Aaron hadn't even grabbed his shoulder again. "But it doesn't make any sense..."

"In *his* eyes we failed," Aaron said.

"In your eyes, too," Whit admitted. "It was what you thought. You don't think that's really Stanley Jessup out there?"

Aaron was afraid that it was, and he was afraid that he had left Charlotte out there alone with the madman.

WITH ALL THE shots flying, Charlotte had no way of knowing if Aaron had made it safely inside the house. She had heard breaking glass. Was it from bullets or from a body flying through a window?

It was too dark for her to see anything. And tonight there wasn't even a sliver of the moon that had been out the previous evening. She could see nothing of the house. Or the gunman.

Was it only one? Was it Stanley Jessup?

Josie had been so convinced that her dad was a good man. But he had made enemies—with the stories he'd run on all his media outlets. Good men didn't make enemies, did they?

But then even if he was a good man, he could have let his grief and loss drive him over the edge. If all that mattered to him now was vengeance, he wouldn't rest until both Whit and Aaron were dead.

Maybe Whit was already dead.

Aaron would be devastated if he was. Just as he had blamed himself for Josie's death, he would blame himself for Whit's. Maybe even more so because they had been estranged, their friendship destroyed because of her.

She was the one whom Aaron needed to blame. Not himself. The burden of guilt should be hers to bear—not his.

If he wanted to kill the person responsible for him losing his daughter, Jessup should be trying to kill her—not them. She moved around the back of the car and kept low behind the hedges that lined the driveway. She made it to the garage. Her foot struck some shells, sending them skittering across the asphalt.

This was where the man had been standing when he'd fired round after round at the Camaro. And at her and Aaron. Where had he gone?

She clutched her gun in her hand and spun around, looking for him.

"Over here, Charlotte," a gruff voice murmured.

Whose voice? Whit's? It wasn't Aaron because her pulse didn't quicken. Charlotte's heart didn't warm with hope and love. And the baby didn't move in her womb in reaction to her father's voice.

"You looked." The voice was closer now and clearer as the man taunted her. "When I said your name, you looked. I knew it was you." He hid yet in the shadows. "Just from the way you held a gun, I knew it was you."

"Trigger."

All of her lies had destroyed Aaron's trust so much that he had begun to suspect everyone of having ulterior motives. But her gut—and maybe the baby moving inside it—had convinced her it was her old partner.

"That Timmer guy made me doubt myself though," he admitted. "So I went back to Serenity House and talked to the administrator—flashed my U.S. Marshal badge to get her talking."

"She wouldn't have told you anything," Charlotte said, remembering how stubborn that woman had been.

"She didn't realize she was telling me anything," he said, his voice still taunting her from the darkness. "She just answered my questions about your scars. Well, her face answered them with her reaction. She just confirmed what I already knew though."

She didn't bother trying to deny who she was. She just asked, "Did you hurt the man inside the house?"

"What man? The old, rich guy left a while ago," he said.

So maybe he didn't even know about Whit. Maybe that could work to their advantage. If the men realized she needed help in time...

Before it was too late...

"I waited here for you and Timmer to come back," Trigger said. "My source with the state police department told me that they let you two go but arrested some royal subject and his goon bodyguard. So I figured you two would be heading back."

"Then you waited for us and started shooting?" she asked. "What if you'd hit me? How was I going to tell you what you wanted to know then?"

"They don't call me Trigger for nothing," he said with unearned arrogance. "I know how to handle a gun. I only shoot what I mean to."

She could have argued that point with examples. But she just nodded—regardless of whether or not he could see the motion in the dark. "What about those men in the administrator's office? Weren't you worried about them shooting me?"

He chuckled. "What would make you think I had anything to do with that? Didn't they kill that woman?"

"After you questioned her about me," she pointed out. "You spooked her. That's why she was destroying records when we got to her office. That's why you killed her, so she wouldn't admit that she already talked to a U.S. Marshal. Were you trying to get rid of any trace that you'd even been there? That you'd even tracked me down?"

"That lady didn't really matter one way or the other," he said offhandedly. "I told the guys to take the shot if they got it."

How had a lawman become so callous about life? Was it that they had faked so many witnesses' deaths that he didn't realize that some deaths were *real*?

"And me?" she asked.

"They weren't supposed to shoot you," he assured her. "I just paid them to get rid of the men with you."

"Those men are better than you realized," she said with pride. "Or maybe you knew how good they are and that's why you hired the guys but stayed out of the line of fire yourself." Even now he stubbornly stayed in the shadows, so that she couldn't get a clear shot at him. He was both a bully and a coward.

He chuckled again. "They can't help you now."

Her heart slammed into her ribs. Had he killed them? Was it already too late for her to save the man she loved? Was it too late for her to tell Aaron that she loved him?

Her feelings probably wouldn't matter to him. But she needed to say the words—needed to let him know how much he meant to her. And she needed the chance to tell him.

It didn't matter that she didn't have the shot. She lifted her gun to fire into the darkness.

"I wouldn't do that," Trigger warned. And he finally stepped from the shadows. Or at least he dissipated the darkness when he screwed back in the bulb of the porch light under which he stood. His gun wasn't pointed at her though.

She could have taken the shot. But Trigger was Trigger *Happy*. His finger was already pressed to the trigger of his gun while the barrel of it was pressed against Aaron's temple.

"I know you, Charlotte," he said. "There was no way in hell you would tell me what I want to know to save yourself. I could press this gun to your head and you would let me pull the trigger before you'd ever give me the location of the witness."

She nodded. "True. I won't reveal the location of a witness." Any witness, but most especially one with whom she'd bonded like she had Josie. It was no wonder that Aaron had fallen for the woman. She was smart and funny and sweet. And she deserved to live her life in peace—not with the constant threat of danger.

"But I think if it comes down between his life and hers, you'll pick his," Trigger said.

Aaron laughed. "You don't know her as well as you think you do."

"I think you're the one who doesn't know her," Trigger said. "She loves you. Even when she didn't really know who *she* was, Dr. Platt confirmed the amnesia wasn't a trick, Charlotte knew that she loved you."

She had wanted Aaron to know her feelings, but she'd wanted to be the one to tell him. And how had Trigger so easily recognized what had taken her so long to realize?

"I saw it on her face," he continued talking to Aaron. "She won't let me kill you."

The guy was a hell of a lot smarter than Charlotte had given him credit for.

"So before I pull this trigger," Trigger warned her, "you better tell me what I need to know. Where is Josie Jessup?"

Need to. Not want to know…

This was about more than money to Trigger, which made him even more desperate and dangerous. He would pull that trigger.

"Don't tell him," Aaron said. "Let him shoot!"

Charlotte flinched with the realization that the man she loved still loved another woman—so much that he was willing to give up his life for hers.

But Charlotte wasn't willing to make that sacrifice.

Aaron might never be hers. But he belonged to someone else—he was the father of the baby she carried.

And he would be a good father—the kind of father a little girl needed.

"I'll tell you," she said. "I'll tell you what you want to know."

IT WAS A trick. Charlotte Green wouldn't give up the location of a witness. Not for her own life. And not for anyone else's.

Aaron knew that as well as the U.S. Marshal did. The older man tensed and buried the barrel of his gun even deeper into the skin of Aaron's temple.

"You're going to tell me?" Trigger asked, his voice cracking with suspicion. "Really?"

"Let him go," she negotiated, "and I'll tell you."

Trigger laughed. "You always treated me like I'm an idiot. You really think I'm going to take your word that'll you tell me where she is once I release my leverage?"

"Do you think it matters?" Aaron asked. "Do you really think she's going to give you Josie's real location? She could tell you anywhere. Could set you up to walk into a booby-trapped house and get your head blown off. You just said she thinks you're an idiot." He snorted. "Sounds like she's right to think that."

"Aaron—" she protested.

It probably wasn't his smartest move to goad the man holding a gun to his head. But then he'd never been all that smart where Charlotte was involved.

Apparently neither had Trigger since the guy actually thought she loved Aaron. Sure, she was attracted to him. Their attraction was so strong that the air between them fairly sizzled when they got close. But love was something else. Love implied need. And Charlotte

Green had never needed anyone. She took independence and self-sufficiency to an extreme.

"You better not give me the wrong location," Trigger threatened. "Because I'm bringing him with me and if your directions don't lead me to Josie Jessup, he'll get that bullet in his head."

That had no doubt been his plan all along—to put a bullet in his head and one in Charlotte's, too. He couldn't leave behind any witnesses.

But he couldn't kill Charlotte until he knew for certain she'd given him the correct location.

Charlotte lifted her hands above her head, as if she were being held up. "All right, I'll tell you the truth."

She met Aaron's gaze, hers dark with frustration. And something else…pain.

How had he hurt her? He was trying to help her. Didn't she realize?

"Ironically she's not that far from here," she said. "She's in Michigan, too." She named a city just a few hours north of where they were. Then she added a number and a street name.

Trigger grabbed Aaron's arm and jerked him along with him, dragging him toward his vehicle. But the gun never left his temple. It would no doubt leave a mark even if the guy didn't shoot.

"You can't take him with you," Charlotte protested. "I gave you what you wanted."

"But as the man pointed out, you can't be trusted, Charlotte." He pushed Aaron through the passenger's side of his car, keeping his gun barrel tight against his temple. "He's my insurance that you're telling the truth. If you are, I might let him live."

The barrel vibrated as the man laughed with amusement over his own sick joke. "And if you are lying to me," Trigger said, "I'll be back. I'll find you again. And the next person I'll take away from you will be your kid."

Charlotte gasped with obvious fear, and her palm protectively covered her belly.

"It'd be a shame for him to be raised without a father anyway," Trigger said, turning the proverbial knife. "Look what it did to you."

Aaron saw the pain cross Charlotte's face, and he wanted to hurt Trigger for hurting her. He wanted to make the man suffer as he was making her suffer.

Didn't she realize that Aaron had a plan? Didn't she trust him?

No. She wouldn't tell him where Josie was. She wouldn't even tell him where Princess Gabriella was. He doubted she had given Trigger the real location. Maybe that was the reason for the pained look on her face.

Guilt.

She thought she had sealed his death warrant.

Aaron tried to catch her attention, tried, with his gaze, to convince her not to worry. But then he did have a gun pressed to his head. And the U.S. Marshal's real nickname wasn't just Trigger. But Happy...

He was laughing yet, still amused by his sick joke. He shoved the barrel harder into Aaron's skin. "Start the car, damn it!"

He obliged, turning the key and shifting it from Park to Drive.

"And no crazy stunt driving like the other night," Trigger warned, pressing a hand over the bump on his forehead.

"That wasn't me," Aaron assured him. "That was my friend. Whit."

Trigger's brow furrowed. "The guy who got shot at the administrator's office?"

Aaron nodded, knocking the barrel a little loose.

"I'm glad the son of a bitch got shot then."

Aaron pressed on the accelerator, easing the car away from where Charlotte stood, staring helplessly after them.

"She really loves you," Trigger remarked. "Didn't think the ice princess had it in her. But she gave up the witness location."

"How do you know it's the real one?" he asked again, wanting the guy to be doubtful and nervous.

"You better hope it is," Trigger threatened, "or you'll be paying the price for her lies."

"Maybe you'll be paying the price," Aaron remarked. "It could still be a trap. That place is three hours away— gives her three hours to have authorities in place to grab you."

"We're not going there," Trigger said, fishing a phone out of his pocket. "All I needed was to get the address. I don't need to go there."

Aaron glanced into the rearview mirror where Charlotte's figure was getting smaller and smaller. She stood there when she needed to be getting on the phone, needed to be getting Josie to safety.

Unless she'd done as Aaron had suspected, given Trigger a false address.

"So this person who must be paying you a pretty penny, he or she won't be upset if you send them into a trap?"

"What?"

"Like I said, you really don't think Charlotte Green gave up the actual location of a witness…especially one she considers a friend?"

Trigger glanced back, too—just distracted enough that he gave Aaron a chance to reach for the gun. But they barely grappled with it before a shot rang out—shattering the windshield.

And ending a life...

Chapter Fifteen

The gunshot shattered the eerie silence that had fallen once the car pulled down the driveway of the rental house. Brake lights flashed on that car, and a horn blared.

A scream tore from Charlotte's throat. He'd shot Aaron. He'd shot him.

She'd thought Aaron had had a plan. That was the only reason she'd let them pull away. Otherwise she might have risked a shot; she would have tried to hit her old partner. But with his finger already on the trigger, there was no way he wouldn't have pulled it—even if just by reflex.

But at least then she would have had the satisfaction of taking out the Marshal herself. A satisfaction she still intended to have.

Tears streaming down her face like rain off a rock, she ran down the driveway—heading toward the stopped car. She bypassed the driver's side. She couldn't see Aaron—like she'd seen those other shooting victims. Instead she headed toward the passenger's side, jerked open the door and pointed her gun inside. Her finger trembled as she moved to squeeze the trigger.

"You can't kill him twice," a male voice remarked. The man sprawled in the backseat.

And Trigger slumped over the dash, a bullet in his head and his blood sprayed across the shattered windshield.

"Aaron!" she screamed his name, trying to peer around the other man to the driver's side. But it was empty—no one sitting behind the wheel.

Then warm hands closed over her shoulders, twirling her toward him—pulling her tight against a strong chest. "Shh…" a deep voice murmured into her ear.

She shivered and trembled in reaction to the horror she had just endured over thinking him dead. "You're alive!"

"I'm fine," he assured her.

But blood had spattered the side of his face when Whit had killed Trigger. Seeing it on his face had her stomach lurching with fear over what could have happened, over how that blood could have been his.

She pulled back and swung her palm at him, striking his shoulder hard enough to propel him back a couple of steps. "You're an idiot! How could you do that? How could you risk your life that way?"

"We had a plan," Whit said. His face twisted into a grimace of pain as he crawled from the backseat and joined them on the driveway.

"What kind of plan?" she asked, anger eclipsing her earlier relief. "A suicide pact?"

Whit pointed toward the front seat. "Only one who wound up dead was the bad guy."

She stared hard at the king's blond bodyguard. Even though she had worked with him to stage Josie's murder, she hadn't trusted him. Maybe because he'd agreed to keep a secret from a man he'd claimed was his best friend.

"I'm really not a bad guy," he said.

She threw her arms around him, hugging him tight. He grunted with pain.

And Aaron protested, "Why are you hugging him? I'm the one who risked my life."

"You're not helping your cause with that," Whit said, as he awkwardly patted Charlotte's back. "I think that could be why she's pissed at you."

"Well, I'm not exactly thrilled with her, either," Aaron admitted.

"Lovers' spat?" Whit teased.

"She doesn't just know where Josie is," Aaron said. "She knows where Princess Gabriella is too."

Whit's hands clenched on Charlotte's shoulders, pulling her back. "You know? Have you known all along?"

She uttered a shaky sigh and stepped back—away from both angry men. "Just since my memory returned."

"Since then?" Whit seemed more appalled than Aaron had been.

Aaron had just seemed betrayed. It would be a miracle if he ever trusted her again. And now that he knew where Josie was...

She expected him to leave soon. She glanced inside the car again. "We need to call the police."

"And probably Stanley Jessup's lawyer," Aaron added. "To help us explain everything that's happened and how a U.S. Marshal wound up dead."

"I had to shoot him," Whit said, "or he was going to kill you."

That feeling of panic and loss struck Charlotte again. She had nearly lost him. Not that she still wasn't going to lose him. He would be a part of his child's life. But he probably wouldn't be a part of hers.

And that was fine. She had never envisioned for herself the fairy-tale, happily-ever-after ending.

"You saved my life," Aaron said, and patted his friend's shoulder in appreciation.

Whit groaned in pain. "Damn it! Stop doing that!"

"I'll leave the two of you alone," Charlotte said, "to bond again." But she didn't make it two steps before Whit stopped her, with his hand on her arm.

"You're going to tell me where Gabby is."

She shook her head. "I haven't talked to her in six months. I need to make certain she still is where I sent her. And I have to find out if she's ready to see anyone yet."

"It's been six months," Whit reiterated. "Why would she need more time before she would want to see anyone?"

"She felt betrayed," Charlotte reminded him. "She's hurt and she's scared. And it may take more than six months for her to get over it." Because she suspected it would take more than six months for Aaron to get over her betraying him.

"I'll call her," she offered. Actually now that the threat against Gabriella was gone, Charlotte couldn't wait to see her sister again. They had so much to talk about—like the fact that Gabby was going to be an aunt.

Hell, she didn't even know that Charlotte was her sister. The king had forbidden her to tell the younger woman the truth. He hadn't thought Gabby was strong enough to handle that, but he'd had no problem passing her from potential bridegroom to potential bridegroom.

Charlotte should have ignored his threat to fire her if she told the truth. Because, by keeping that secret, she had betrayed the princess just as everyone else had. Charlotte was done keeping secrets; it was time for her to be honest with her sister. It was too late for her to be honest with Aaron.

As she headed toward the house, she felt both men watching her. With resentment...

And her heart ached with loss. Aaron was alive, but he would never be hers.

"GOD, THAT WOMAN is infuriating!" Whit exclaimed, staring after Charlotte.

"Yes, she is," Aaron agreed wholeheartedly, as he rubbed the blood off his face.

Whit slapped him on the shoulder now. "You're a lucky man."

"What?" His friend must have lost more blood that he'd thought. "Are you okay?"

"Yeah," Whit assured him, "I'm just a little jealous. Okay, a lot jealous."

He studied his friend's face. Dawn was approaching, lightening the dark sky, so that he could see more clearly now. Apparently more clearly than Whit could see. "You're not making any sense."

"She loves you," Whit said.

"What?" he asked. Whit must have heard Trigger's claims and believed the madman.

Whit slapped his shoulder again. "Is that one more thing she kept from you? Her feelings?"

"She doesn't love me," Aaron insisted. "She doesn't even trust me." And how could you love someone you couldn't trust? The thought made his heart ache with loss.

Whit blew out a ragged breath. "She gave up Josie's whereabouts for your life."

Aaron shook his head. "No. She must have made up that address she gave him—just to buy us all some time to get Trigger under control."

Whit shook his head. "No. That is really Josie's address." Whit must have had the window cracked when he'd crouched down in the backseat of Trigger's car.

"No one but Charlotte knows where she stashed Josie," Aaron reminded him. That was why the U.S. Marshal had gone to such extremes to get the information from her. "So how would you know if she told me the truth or not?"

"I followed her the day that she moved Josie," Whit admitted.

"You really cared about her?"

"Not as much as you did, but yeah," Whit said. "She was an amazing lady."

"Is," he corrected him even though he was still getting used to the idea himself of Josie Jessup being alive. He'd wasted more than three years on guilt and anger.

"You never acted on your feelings for her," Whit said with absolute certainty. They hadn't taken shifts but had watched her together.

"She was a client," Aaron reminded him. "We were paid to protect her." And he would never cross that line.

"Her protection was why I followed Charlotte that day—to make sure that no one else followed them."

And that was why Aaron had struggled to understand why Whit had talked him into leaving the safe house the day it had exploded. Because he had always been vigilant about protecting their clients.

Whit nodded. "I had to make sure that Josie would be safe."

"Charlotte made sure of that," Aaron pointed out. So he could no longer resent her for keeping that secret from him. She'd just been doing her job. Actually she'd gone above and beyond because Josie had become a friend of hers. No matter how tough and independent she acted, Charlotte allowed herself to get close. To be vulnerable…

"Charlotte was kind of a client, wasn't she?" Whit asked, as if testing his former partner. "Being the king's daughter and all."

"I didn't know that she was," he reminded Whit and himself of another secret to which he hadn't been privy. And his resentment returned.

"Doesn't matter if you knew that or not, I guess," Whit continued. "As the princess's doppelganger bodyguard, she was still part of the job detail."

Wondering where his friend was heading with his comments, Aaron only nodded his agreement.

"And yet you acted on your feelings for her," Whit said.

Aaron arched a brow, wondering how Whit knew.

"Her kid is yours, right?"

Aaron nodded and then grinned with overwhelming, fatherly pride. "Yes."

"So your feelings for her are obviously stronger than your feelings were for Josie," Whit concluded.

"Josie was a friend," Aaron said.

"And Charlotte?"

His everything. "I don't know what she is. Or how she feels."

"She loves you."

Aaron's heart warmed with hope, but he didn't dare believe Whit's declaration. He wouldn't believe it until Charlotte herself told him her feelings.

But he suspected that was another secret she wasn't willing to share.

GABRIELLA HADN'T ANSWERED. But the phone hadn't rang and rang, either. Instead Charlotte had heard a message that the number she'd dialed was no longer a working exchange. It probably meant nothing more than that the minutes had run out on the disposable cell Charlotte had given her.

But who had Gabriella been calling? No one else knew where she was. And the few who'd thought they had, had actually mistaken Charlotte for the princess.

Unless Gabriella had used those minutes trying to reach her. When the men had burst into the hotel suite in Paris, she had destroyed her phone—making certain that there had been no way those men could track down the real princess. "Where are you?" she asked aloud, her voice echoing in the eerie quiet of the bedroom where she and Aaron had made love just hours before. The sheets were still tangled and scented with the sexy musk of Aaron's skin. Of their lovemaking…

She trembled with need. But it was a need she suspected would go unanswered. He was probably already on his way to Josie.

"Here you are," a deep voice murmured.

She glanced up to find him in the doorway, leaning against the jamb and studying her. "You were looking for me?" she asked and then realized his probable reason why. "Are the police here?"

"On their way," he confirmed. "So is someone else."

So instead of going to her, he was bringing Josie to him? That was even more dangerous.

"You called her? You can't do that," she said. "Someone could have traced the call. You could have put her in danger."

"Her who?" he asked, his brow furrowing with confusion. He still bore the round mark of the barrel of

Trigger's gun on his temple. "I don't know where Gabriella is."

"Not Gabby," she said, "Josie. You can't call Josie."

"Of course I can't," he agreed. "I don't have her number," he said.

Relief shuddered through her, and she hated herself that she wasn't just relieved her friend was safe but relieved that Aaron hadn't immediately tried to contact her. She hated this petty jealousy. It had to be the pregnancy hormones making her so emotional and crazy— because she had never acted like this before. But then she had never been in love before, either.

"I didn't even know I really had her address until now," he said.

She waited for him to leave then—to rush off to the woman he really loved. But he stayed where he was, staring at her so intently it was as if he was trying to see inside her.

"What?" She self-consciously lifted trembling fingers and ran them across her cheek. But the scar wasn't there anymore. She had nothing to run her fingertips along like she used to.

"Why did you give him her real address?" he asked, all narrow-eyed curiosity.

She shrugged, but the tension didn't leave her shoulders. She knew why she had. "I couldn't risk your life."

"But by telling him, you risked hers."

Guilt and regret clutched at her. She hated that she'd done that—hated that she'd been so weak.

"Why would you do that?" he asked.

"I—I shouldn't have done that," she regretfully admitted. "I shouldn't have told him."

"Trigger is dead," he assured her—a slight shudder moving his broad shoulders as he must have relived that moment when Whit had shot the man holding a gun to Aaron's head. "It doesn't matter now what you told him."

She released a shuddery breath. "True. It doesn't matter."

"Except it does," he said. "To me."

He was asking a question she was too afraid to answer. Earlier she'd thought that she should tell him her feelings—that she should because if something had happened to him, she would want him to know that she loved him.

But Trigger was dead. The prince and his henchman arrested. Nothing was going to happen to Aaron. But something bad could happen to her. She could tell him she loved him, and he could reject her.

So she cast around for any reason that she could keep her feelings to herself, like the fact that he loved another woman. "Now that you know where she is, are you going to go see her?"

"And risk someone following me?" He shook his head. "I wouldn't put a friend's life at risk."

Like she had.

"A friend?" The question slipped out, and she hoped it didn't reveal her jealousy. "Is that all Josie is to you?"

He nodded. "We were friends when she *died*."

"Just friends?" she asked. "You gave up your business because of what happened to her."

"What I thought happened to her," he said. "I didn't think I was too good at my job then so giving it up seemed like the right thing."

"And Whit?"

"I guess, subconsciously, I knew he was keeping something from me," Aaron said. "So I didn't trust him.

I didn't want anything to do with someone I couldn't trust."

And that was her reason for not telling him her feelings. He didn't trust her. After all the secrets she'd kept from him, she didn't blame him; she wouldn't trust her, either.

Since she had given up a witness's location, no one could trust her. Maybe it was good that she hadn't gotten in touch with Gabriella. The princess was safer without Charlotte knowing exactly where she was.

Sirens in the distance drew her attention. And she remembered something else he'd said. "Who, besides the police, is on their way?" she asked. "Stanley Jessup's lawyer?"

They would probably need him to help clean up and explain the mess they'd made in this small Michigan town. She doubted anyone would believe their convoluted tale of doppelgangers and kidnappings and amnesia and royalty.

"King St. Pierre is on his way," Aaron said.

Panic struck her. She was in no condition to deal with that man. Not now. Maybe not ever again. "What?"

"I called him," Aaron explained. "He needs to know what's going on."

"Why?" she asked. "So he can fire all of us?"

"You're his daughter."

She laughed. "Not to him, I'm not. I'm just an employee—like the two of you. You two were hired to protect him, and instead you came here—"

"He wanted us to find the princess," Aaron said. "He was all right with using his old security detail again. Why did you want them replaced?"

"I wanted you and Whit to work together again," she said. But she couldn't take all the credit with a clear conscience. "Actually Josie suggested it. She felt bad that her needing to disappear caused a rift in your friendship."

He grinned with obvious affection for the other woman. Just friends? Really?

"But I didn't entirely trust his current people, either," she admitted. "Especially Zeke Rogers." The former mercenary had given off a bad vibe. "The king hadn't done a very good job vetting them."

Kind of like how he hadn't done a very good job of vetting future sons-in-law—putting Gabriella and Charlotte in danger.

"Rogers headed up the king's security detail for years," Aaron said.

"That's why he should have had them more thoroughly checked out," she said. "He didn't know their backgrounds—their vulnerabilities."

"He knows ours now," Aaron said with a heavy sigh. "Guess that Whit and I can start up our business again if he fires us."

"He will," Charlotte warned him. "You found him the wrong daughter."

Just like she was the wrong woman for Aaron. She couldn't tell him her feelings. But it was okay. She had her baby. She would give her all her love.

Chapter Sixteen

Aaron waited for it but the words didn't come. So he asked the older man point-blank, "You're not firing me?"

Using Whit's gunshot wound as an excuse, Aaron had taken the meeting alone with the king. The gray-haired man paced the den of Stanley Jessup's rental home. His gaze kept going to the blood smeared on the leather couch. "Why would I fire you?"

"I followed this lead on my own," he sheepishly reminded him. He'd put himself in danger because he'd trusted the wrong people and hadn't trusted the right ones.

The king absolved him of any culpability, just as Stanley Jessup had. "You didn't think you could trust anyone."

"But shouldn't I have trusted you?" Aaron asked. Maybe he wanted to get fired. Because if Charlotte wasn't working at the palace, he had no reason for being there.

The king shrugged but even that had a regal edge to it. "Charlotte doesn't trust me."

"She probably won't tell you where Gabriella is," Aaron admitted. "But it's just to keep her safe." He believed that now, where before he'd thought it might have been out of spite that she wouldn't tell her father where his chosen daughter was.

But given how the first man to whom Rafael had promised his daughter had nearly killed Charlotte, he didn't trust the man's judgment. Even if arranging marriages was fine in his realm, Aaron hated to think of anyone marrying for any reason but love.

That was why he hadn't already asked Charlotte. He didn't want to marry her just because they were about to have a child together. He wanted to marry her for the reason his own blissfully happy parents had married— true love.

"You are a loyal man," the king praised him. "I will not fire you or Whit Howell. I believe it is my good fortune to have you as part of my security detail."

"And what about Charlotte?" he asked. Would he fire her as she suspected?

"She is not just a bodyguard," the king said. "She is my daughter."

Aaron was surprised by the man's admission. "You're claiming her now?"

Rafael St. Pierre's shoulders sagged with his heavy burden of guilt and regret. "I should have always claimed her."

"You should have," Aaron wholeheartedly agreed. "You don't deserve her."

"Do you?" the king asked, calling him on his hypocrisy. "I'm assuming you're the father of her baby?" No matter how busy the man had been ruling his country, he must have remained aware of what was going on with his daughters.

Aaron nodded. And now he realized the purpose of

this meeting. Today the king was just a father asking a man his intentions toward his pregnant daughter.

It didn't matter that Aaron, like Charlotte, was in his thirties. Heat rushed to his neck, and nerves mangled his guts—and he was every bit as nervous as a teenager who'd gotten his young girlfriend pregnant.

"I love her," he said. "And I'd like to marry her. But I don't know if she'll have me."

The king was not going to get away with arranging a marriage for his oldest daughter. But if he were to do that, he would undoubtedly choose someone with more wealth and means than Aaron had.

But no one could offer her the love that Aaron could. "I don't know if she can trust anyone to love her."

"Because of me." The king readily took the blame, his shoulders sagging even more with the additional burden. "I will talk to her for you."

Aaron flinched. "Championing me may not help my situation at all." If that had even been the man's intentions...

"She will not listen to me," Rafael agreed, "because she hates me."

Aaron shook his head. "If she hated you, she wouldn't be so hurt that you rejected her."

"I had more reasons for treating her how I did," the king said in his own defense. "But I really had no excuse for putting my country before my child."

Aaron couldn't absolve the man of his guilt—not when his actions had so badly hurt the woman he loved.

"Charlotte deserves to come first," he admonished the man.

The king studied Aaron's face through narrowed eyes. His eyes were a darker shade of brown than his daughters' warm golden brown. "Does she come first with you?" he asked.

"Yes," he answered from his heart.

"Does she know that?" the king wondered.

Given the way she'd treated him earlier, Aaron doubted it.

"Not yet." But he would make certain that she would have no doubts that she was the only woman for him.

CHARLOTTE WAITED OUTSIDE the door to the den where the two most important men in her life were locked inside together.

"Are you worried?" Whit asked and pointed toward the closed door. "About what's going on in there? Do you think your daddy is getting out the shotgun to force Aaron to the altar to make an honest woman of you?"

At the outrageous thought, she uttered a short, bitter chuckle. "I doubt that's happening."

"You don't think your father would defend your honor?" Whit asked.

"No."

"Do you want me to defend your honor?" Whit offered sweetly. "I could rough up Aaron for you."

"Since you only have one arm working right now," she reminded him, "I don't like your chances."

He shrugged then grimaced at his own gesture. "Well, I offered. So what do you think they are talking about in there?"

"Gabriella." That was the only daughter the king would worry about and rightfully so. "I'm worried about her, too," she admitted. "I couldn't reach her on the phone earlier."

All his teasing aside, Whit anxiously asked, "But she should be fine, right?" He nodded in response to his own question. "Of course she's fine. We neutralized all the threats against her."

"She's Princess Gabriella," Charlotte said. "There will always be threats against her."

A muscle twitched in his cheek as he tightly clenched his jaw.

"People will want to kidnap her for her father's money or his power," she said. "She's always in danger. And then there was that note shoved under her door the night of the ball."

"What note?" he snapped, as if he should have seen it himself. As if he'd been with Gabby...

"It threatened her life," she said. "It promised that she would die before she would get the chance to marry Prince Malamatos. It was why we left for Paris the next morning." When Charlotte would have rather stayed and explored her burgeoning feelings for Aaron. But then those feelings had burgeoned even when she'd been away from him.

He expelled a ragged sigh. "That was why you left? It wasn't because she was excited to get a dress for her wedding?"

Charlotte chuckled again—this time with real mirth over Whit's ignorance. "Gabby had no intention of marrying either man her father promised her to."

"That's why you put her in your unofficial relocation program," Whit said with sudden understanding.

"I wanted her safe and happy." And now she wasn't sure she was either anymore.

"So are you going to track her down and make certain she's all right?" Whit asked with an eagerness that revealed his true feelings for the princess.

"No," she said.

He jerked with surprise. "I thought you cared about her?"

"I do," Charlotte insisted. "But I'm not going to track her down, because you are."

He nodded. "Of course, in your condition, you shouldn't be doing a lot of traveling."

She could have pointed out that her condition was a lot healthier than his at the moment. But she skipped it. "I'll tell you where I sent her, and you'll find her and make sure she's all right."

"I'm probably the last person she wants to see," Whit admitted with a heavy sigh of regret.

Charlotte wasn't so sure about that. "Just find her and keep her safe." She pressed a paper into his hand with Gabriella's last itinerary.

Whit clutched the piece of a paper in a tight fist. "If I hadn't already told Aaron he was a lucky man, I'd tell him again."

"Why is Aaron lucky?" she asked.

"Because he has you," Whit said. Without waiting to talk to his employer or friend again, the man turned and headed out the front door.

Before Charlotte had a chance to point out that in order for Aaron to be lucky, he'd actually have to want her. And he'd already said that he couldn't be with someone he couldn't trust.

The door to the den opened, but only one man stepped out. Her father. She braced herself for his anger. For his demands.

She hadn't braced herself for a physical confrontation, for the man throwing his arms around her and pulling her close.

"I thought you were dead," he murmured, his voice cracking with emotion.

Tears stung her eyes at his seemingly genuine and heartfelt relief that she was alive. "I'm fine."

"And I will be forever grateful for that," her father said. "I never should have let you become Gabriella's bodyguard."

She flinched. Here was the rejection she'd expected. The firing she'd anticipated.

"I shouldn't have allowed you to put yourself at risk," he said. "I should have had protection for you, too. But I have remedied that situation. You now have your own bodyguard."

"Who?"

"Me," Aaron said, as he joined them in the hall.

She laughed. "I don't need a bodyguard."

"Then consider him a bodyguard for my heir," the king said.

Charlotte clasped her hands to her belly, as if to protect the child. "You haven't claimed me. How can you claim my baby?"

"That's something else I'm going to remedy," he promised. "I'm claiming you as my daughter. As my firstborn."

She nodded with sudden understanding and soul-stealing disappointment. "Of course. Having me as your legal heir will take Gabriella out of danger."

The king groaned with frustration. "This isn't about her. This is about you—about my finally doing right by you."

"Then don't lie to me," she said. "Don't claim feelings you don't have."

"I've always had the feelings," he said. "I just denied them—for the sake of my wife while she was alive and then for the sake of my honor and my kingdom. But I realized, when I thought you were dead, that none of that mattered anymore."

His wife had been dead for years. But for him to say his honor or kingdom didn't matter…

Could he be telling the truth? Could he actually care about Charlotte?

"Maybe you shouldn't publicly claim her," Aaron said. "As her bodyguard, I think we can keep her safer if no one else knows she's related to you."

The king turned to Charlotte. "I don't want to wait another day to declare you as mine. But I don't want you in danger, either."

"Or is it your heir you're worried about?" she asked. "I think she's a girl. You still won't have that boy you want."

The king shook his head and turned back to Aaron. "I can't get through to her. She's too stubborn." His voice cracked with more of that emotion that seemed to overwhelm him. "I wish you luck with her."

"What did my father mean by that?" Charlotte asked once she and Aaron were alone again in the room they'd shared. "Is he talking about you being my bodyguard? Because that's ridiculous. I don't need a bodyguard."

She needed Aaron though. She needed him for her lover, her friend—her soul mate. But if she couldn't have him as those things, she wouldn't settle for less.

"No, you don't need a bodyguard," Aaron agreed with a slight chuckle. "You need a husband."

"Why? Because I'm pregnant?" She snorted derisively. "That's archaic—kind of like a man arranging a marriage for his daughter." She groaned with sudden realization of the conversation that must have taken place in that den. "He arranged for you to marry me, didn't he?"

"He gave his blessing," Aaron admitted.

And now Charlotte fully understood Gabby's horror at being auctioned off, like a side of beef, for money and power. Aaron could give the king neither of those for her hand, though. But then she had never been the daughter that mattered. He must have been bluffing about claiming her. Maybe he had prearranged with Aaron to reject that idea under the ruse of keeping her safe.

They could keep her safe from danger. But not from pain...

"What did you promise him in exchange for his blessing?" she wondered aloud. Because the king was too shrewd and too mercenary to give up something without receiving something in return—just like her mother had been. No wonder Bonita had been his mistress for so many years—after they'd met at a charity ball at which her missionary parents had been guest speakers.

"I did make him a promise," Aaron admitted, "that I would love you and cherish you the rest of our lives."

Her heart shifted, kicking inside her chest like the baby kicking inside her womb. Her legs trembled and she dropped onto the edge of the bed. "Why would you make a promise you can't keep?"

Why would he give her foolish heart such hope when he couldn't possibly really want to marry her?

AARON DROPPED TO his knees in front of Charlotte and took her hand in both of his. "I don't make promises I can't keep," he said. "You know that. You know me. If you accept my proposal, I will spend the rest of my life loving you. Will you marry me, Charlotte Green?"

"No."

He felt as though she'd kicked him. But as her father

had warned, she was stubborn—and totally convinced that she was unlovable.

"Why not?"

"Because it's not the nineteenth century," she said. "And we don't need to get married just because I'm pregnant."

"I don't want to marry you because you're pregnant," he said. "I want to marry you because I love you."

She still refused to believe him, to believe in herself. "No, you don't."

"Have I ever lied to you?" he asked.

She stilled and shook her head. "No, but...I've lied to you. And you said you wouldn't be with someone you can't trust."

"You lied or kept secrets to protect people." And maybe to protect herself if Whit was right and she actually loved him, too. "Except when you told Trigger where to find Josie. Why did you do that?"

"I told you that I couldn't risk your life."

"Why not?"

She groaned as if in pain, as if she were being tortured for information. And then she made the admission in the same way—begrudgingly, resentfully. "Because I love you."

He fought the grin that tugged at his mouth. He wanted to rejoice in her love. But he couldn't accept it until she could accept his—his love and his proposal. "You can love me but I can't love you?"

"You love Josie Jessup," she said.

"As a friend." He'd already told her this. But it was easier for her to believe that he loved Josie than that he loved her.

"You mourned her like a lover."

"I mourned her because I felt guilty," he admitted.

Then, with sudden realization, he repeated, "I mourned her. But I didn't mourn *you*."

She flinched with pain, and he realized that this had been her problem all along, why she had fought to hide or probably even admit to her feelings for him. She had believed him in love with another woman. She'd felt second best again, like she had to her sister.

"I didn't mourn you because I knew you weren't dead," he explained. "Everyone else tried to convince me that you were. Whit—"

"My dad?"

He nodded.

"You have more respect for my skills," she said.

He shook his head. "You're amazing, but that wasn't the reason. I knew that I would have felt it if you had died. Because there's this connection between us—this bond that I've never had with anyone else—not Josie. Not Whit."

He entwined his fingers with hers. "I knew you were alive because I could feel your heart beating. Thousands of miles separated us, but I could feel your heart beating in my heart. We are that connected."

Her breath caught, and her beautiful eyes shimmered with tears. "Aaron..."

"Do you feel it, too?" he asked. "Do you feel this connection between us? Between our souls?"

She nodded. "You are my soul mate."

"So I am going to ask you again," he warned her. "Will you marry me? Will you make me the happiest man in the world for the rest of our lives?"

"Yes, I will," she said with a smile of pure joy.

She wound her arms around his neck and pulled him close. And just as he'd said, her heart pounded against his—inside his, as if they were one. He felt her happiness, too, as it filled him with the warmth of joy and love and relief that she had finally accepted his proposal. But more important, he knew that she had accepted his love.

Her mouth pressed quick kisses to his lips and his cheek and the side of his nose. "I will marry you," she clarified, as if he could have mistaken her intentions. "And I will spend the rest of my life making you happy."

"You already have," he said. "By giving me your love and our child."

"Our child..." Those tears shimmered even more brightly in her eyes. "*You* gave me our child," she said. "You gave me the family I never had. You have already made me the happiest woman in the world."

A thought occurred to him and Aaron chuckled with sudden amusement.

"What?" she asked, her smile still full and bright. She looked more like her sister now—younger and more carefree and optimistic.

"It's a good thing Whit didn't hear any of this," he shared his thought. "He would tease us mercilessly for being hopeless romantics."

She chuckled, too, but then she said, "We might not be the only ones."

"Whit? A hopeless romantic?" He snorted at the ridiculous notion. He had never met a more cynical person—until he'd met Charlotte. If she could let herself fall in love...

Maybe it was possible that Whitaker Howell could find happiness, too.

"Since I will no longer keep any secrets from you," she vowed, "I need to tell you that I sent him to find Gabriella."

Aaron tensed with concern for his fiancée's sister. "Do you think she's in danger?"

"As the king's daughter, she's always in danger," she reminded him.

It was why Aaron preferred that the king not acknowledge her now or maybe ever. He hated the thought of people coming after her because of her father. But then Trigger had already come after her because of who she was. Charlotte could take care of herself though. Despite what she had taught her sister, he wasn't so sure that Princess Gabriella could protect herself.

In that interest of full disclosure to which she now endearingly subscribed, she warned him, "Going to her may put Whit in danger, too."

"He can handle himself." Even after a bullet had ripped through his shoulder, the man had saved their lives.

"He can handle armed gunmen and thugs," she agreed. "I'm not sure he can handle Gabby. She might hurt him. I don't know that she can go against her father's wishes to marry another man."

It hadn't occurred to him that Whit might have been so concerned about Gabby because he'd developed feelings for her. For so long he had believed his friend hadn't possessed any feelings. "Well, I don't know if Whit can protect himself from a broken heart."

Aaron hadn't been able to protect himself from that pain—when he'd thought Charlotte could never trust him and therefore never love him.

As if she'd felt that pain, sadness momentarily dimmed her eyes. "I'm sorry I hurt you," she said, "with all my secrets."

"You had your reasons."

"Not anymore," she said and repeated her earlier vow. "There will be no more secrets between us."

There would be nothing between them anymore but love.

* * * * *

REQUEST YOUR FREE BOOKS!
2 FREE NOVELS PLUS 2 FREE GIFTS!

❖HARLEQUIN®

INTRIGUE®

BREATHTAKING ROMANTIC SUSPENSE

YES! Please send me 2 FREE Harlequin Intrigue® novels and my 2 FREE gifts (gifts are worth about $10). After receiving them, if I don't wish to receive any more books, I can return the shipping statement marked "cancel." If I don't cancel, I will receive 6 brand-new novels every month and be billed just $4.49 per book in the U.S. or $5.24 per book in Canada. That's a savings of at least 14% off the cover price! It's quite a bargain! Shipping and handling is just 50¢ per book in the U.S. and 75¢ per book in Canada.* I understand that accepting the 2 free books and gifts places me under no obligation to buy anything. I can always return a shipment and cancel at any time. Even if I never buy another book, the two free books and gifts are mine to keep forever.

182/382 HDN FVQV

Name	(PLEASE PRINT)	
Address		Apt. #
City	State/Prov.	Zip/Postal Code

Signature (if under 18, a parent or guardian must sign)

Mail to the **Harlequin® Reader Service:**
IN U.S.A.: P.O. Box 1867, Buffalo, NY 14240-1867
IN CANADA: P.O. Box 609, Fort Erie, Ontario L2A 5X3
**Are you a subscriber to Harlequin Intrigue books
and want to receive the larger-print edition?
Call 1-800-873-8635 or visit www.ReaderService.com.**

* Terms and prices subject to change without notice. Prices do not include applicable taxes. Sales tax applicable in N.Y. Canadian residents will be charged applicable taxes. Offer not valid in Quebec. This offer is limited to one order per household. Not valid for current subscribers to Harlequin Intrigue books. All orders subject to credit approval. Credit or debit balances in a customer's account(s) may be offset by any other outstanding balance owed by or to the customer. Please allow 4 to 6 weeks for delivery. Offer available while quantities last.

Your Privacy—The Harlequin® Reader Service is committed to protecting your privacy. Our Privacy Policy is available online at www.ReaderService.com or upon request from the Harlequin Reader Service.

We make a portion of our mailing list available to reputable third parties that offer products we believe may interest you. If you prefer that we not exchange your name with third parties, or if you wish to clarify or modify your communication preferences, please visit us at www.ReaderService.com/consumerschoice or write to us at Harlequin Reader Service Preference Service, P.O. Box 9062, Buffalo, NY 14269. Include your complete name and address.

HI13

Jenna Stark has been on the run for three years, but she'll do anything to protect her son. Even rely on the one man she thought she'd never see again....

The doors squealed open and she stumbled down the steps. Looking both ways, she hopped into the street.

Gavin wailed, "I wanna snowboard."

She jogged to the sidewalk, glancing over her shoulder. Was the man by the truck looking her way?

What now? She hadn't gotten too far from her house... and Marti's dead body. She couldn't go back. She couldn't get her car—the mechanic just got the part this morning.

Think, Jenna.

She couldn't put any more lives in danger. She'd have to hop another bus and get to the main bus depot in Salt Lake City. She had cash...lots of cash. She could get them two tickets to anywhere.

Hitching Gavin higher on her hip, she strode down the snow-dusted street in the opposite direction of the truck— like a woman with purpose. Like a woman with confidence and not in fear for her life.

She turned the next corner, her mind clicking through the streets of Lovett Peak, searching her memory bank for the nearest bus stop.

"Where are we going, Mommy?"

"Someplace warm, honey bunny."

Half a mile away, in front of the high school. That bus could get them to Salt Lake.

She'd start over. Build a new life. Again.

She straightened her spine and marched through the residential streets on her way to the local high school.

When the sound of a loud engine rumbled behind them,

her heartbeat quickened along with her steps as she glanced over her shoulder at an older-model blue car.

When the car slowed down, its engine growling like a predatory animal, she broke into a run.

She heard the door fly open and a man shouted, "Jenna, stop!"

She stumbled, nearly falling to her knees. She'd know that voice anywhere. It belonged to the man responsible for her life on the run.

Cade Stark.

Her husband.

Don't miss the heart-stopping reunion between two people—a spy and a single mom—desperate to give their son a future.

Pick up Carol Ericson's
RUN, HIDE,
on sale in March 2013,
wherever Harlequin Intrigue® books are sold!